THE BREAKER OF STARS
A The Curse of Ophelia Novella

NICOLE PLATANIA

Books by Nicole Platania

The Curse of Ophelia Series

The Curse of Ophelia
The Shards of Ophelia
The Trials of Ophelia
The Breaker of Stars (A Novella)

The *Breaker* of Stars

Nicole Platania

Stars Inked Press, Inc.

6320 Topanga Cyn Blvd. Ste. 1630 #1033

Woodland Hills, CA 91367

First paperback edition July 2024

© Cover design: Franziska Stern - www.coverdungeon.com - Instagram: @coverdungeonrabbit

Copyedited by Grey Moth Editing

Proofread by K. Morton Editing Services

Proofread by Len's Library

Map design by Abigail Hair

ISBN 979-8-9862704-8-7 (Paperback)

ASIN B0CT92RX6R (Ebook)

www.nicoleplatania.com

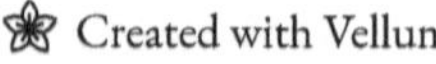 Created with Vellum

To everyone who has found themselves caged.
Your will is stronger than iron.

Author's Note

This book contains depictions of mental/emotional abuse and neglect, mentions of torture, violence, blood/gore, organized fighting, physical ailments related to seizures, and explicit sexual content. If any of these may be triggering for you, please read carefully, or feel free to contact the author for further explanation.

GALLANTIA
AMBRISK
CAPRECION
VALYN
MYSTIQUE
TERRITORIES
LUMIN
LAKE
SPIRIT
VOLCANO
TUNDRA
WILD
PLAINS
STARSEARCHERS
TURREN
DAMENAI
CASTANI
OUTPOST
SOLSTINE RIVER
PALERMAN
XENOVIA
CLIFFS OF BRONTAIN
THE LENDELL HILLS
SOULGUIDERS
SOUTHERN PASS
BODYMELDERS
FIREBIRD
FIELD
SEA WATCHERS'
THORENTIL
FRAUGHTEN RIVER
PTHOLE
WAR
BORDER
LYTAR
TRENCH
MINDSHAPERS
GENNIUM FOREST
SEA WATCHERS
RIVER
GAVERAL
ENGROSSIAN
TERRITORIES
SEA WATCHERS
BANIX

PRONUNCIATION GUIDE

Mystique Warriors

Cypherion Kastroff (he/him), Mystique
    Second: *Sci-fear-ee-on Cast-Rahf*
Ophelia Alabath (she/her), Mystique Revered:
    Oh-feel-eeya Al-uh-bath
Malakai Blastwood (he/him): *Mal-uh-kye Blast-
    wood*
Tolek Vincienzo (he/him): *Tole-ick Vin-chin-zoh*
Jezebel Alabath (she/her): *Jez-uh-bell Al-uh-
    bath*

Starsearchers

Vale (she/her), apprentice: *Veil*
Titus Verian (he/him), Seawatcher Chancellor:
    Tie-tuhs Vair-ee-on
Harlen (he/him): *Har-lin*

Non-warrior characters

Santorina Cordelian (she/her), human: *San-tor-ee-nuh Kor-dee-lee-in*

Animals and Creatures

Erini: *Ih-ree-nee*
Marage: *Mer-ah-guh*

Places

Ambrisk: *Am-brisk*
Castani: *Caah-staw-knee*
Damenal: *Dom-in-all*
Gallantia: *Guh-lawn-shuh*
Lumin: *Loo-min*
Valyn: *Val-in*

Angels of the Gallantian Warriors

Bant (he/him), Prime Engrossian Warrior: *Bant*
Damien (he/him), Prime Mystique Warrior: *Day-mee-in*
Gaveny (he/him), Prime Seawatcher: *Gav-in-ee*
Ptholenix (he/him), Prime Bodymelder: *Tholl-en-icks*
Thorn (he/him), Prime Mindshaper: *Thorn*
Valyrie (she/her), Prime Starsearcher: *Val-er-ee*
Xenique (she/her), Prime Soulguider: *Zen-eek*

Gods of Ambrisk's Pantheon

Aoiflyn (she/her), Fae Goddess: *Eef-lyn*
Artale (she/her), Goddess of Death: *Are-tall*
Gerenth (he/him), God of Nature: *Gair-inth*

Lynxenon (he/him), God of Mythical Beasts:
Leen-zih-non
Moirenna (she/her), Goddess of Fate & Celestial Movements: *Moy-ren-uh*
Thallia (she/her), Witch Goddess of Sorcia:
Thall-ee-uh

Chapter One
Cypherion

One fucking bed.

That was what the tavern owner with the obscenely large ears said. Three times.

I supposed I shouldn't insult his ears; it wasn't their fault the only inn in the tiny northern town of Castani only had one room left.

With one bed.

Narrowing my eyes, I assessed the man behind the bar. Thick arms rested on the wood, a coarse beard masking the bottom half of his expression. But his eyes didn't shift. They didn't avoid my gaze, nor did they light with the challenge of trying to get more coin out of me.

Nothing suspicious, defensive, or calculating.

An uproarious cheer echoed from a table in the corner, bouncing across the wooden tables caged in by foggy glass windows fighting off the winter night. Warriors dotted the rest of the sparsely furnished dining room, the market-based town merely a pass-through for those on their way here or there. The voices echoed in my head, and I gritted my teeth.

Shoving my hand through my hair, I sighed. "Fine. That room will do."

A delicate, stifled laugh sounded behind me, but I didn't look at her. Just pulled the necessary coins from my pouch and dropped them over the bar.

"We left our horses tied out front," I added.

"They'll be cared for as if they belong to the chancellor himself," the owner said. A casual turn of phrase, but one that caused a small intake of breath from my traveling companion. And my damn ears were too attuned to miss it. That, plus the mention of the Starsearcher Chancellor, Titus, had my own muscles locking, fingers itching for one of the many knives beneath my cloak.

Without another word, I turned.

"Thank you," Vale whispered to the owner despite the memories that were certainly inundating her mind now. "May Valyrie bless you."

Even low and directed at another, her voice crawled across my skin, calling to every disgruntled nerve ending, pulling me back to nights I didn't want to relive. Her body beneath mine as she uttered promises she had no intention of keeping. Secrets she'd hidden when I'd come to her, vulnerable and asking for help.

I fisted my hands at my sides to avoid remembering how her skin felt beneath them and reaching—

A low growl rumbled in my throat, and I stopped in my tracks, moving slightly to the side. Without looking directly at Vale, I waited for her to walk in front of me, then continued after her up the creaking wooden staircase.

Curse Ophelia for eternity, these past three weeks had been the hardest of my life, and I'd survived a wide variety of shit thus far.

Leaving my friends at the war camp in the southern mountains to await siege and plot against the now-dead Queen Kakias had been difficult. But the most challenging part was the Starsearcher before me and the battle within my own head. Heart. Whatever.

Not to mention the way every situation appeared to be working against me.

"One fucking bed," I mumbled beneath my breath.

"What was that?" Vale asked, stopping at the landing atop the stairs and flicking a gaze over her shoulder. Those piercing olive-green irises sparkled even in the low light. Eyes I'd seen glazed with tears, fogged during readings, and burning in lust as—

"Nothing." I cleared my throat. "Key?"

Vale lifted a brow, and *Damien's balls,* was she fighting a smirk? That was why I tried not to look at her too often—her face was too expressive. The slightest feeling stole her entire being, something I often wondered about given that she had fucking lied to us for months and no one realized.

Had it been so easy then, to mask her emotions?

Vale rolled her eyes, unlocking the door and leading us into the room. And there it was.

Why did so many inns only have rooms with one bed? This had happened countless times these past three weeks, no matter how often I distinctly asked for two—Spirits, even two separate rooms. Was every warrior on this damn continent currently traveling or were tavern owners too lazy to make up rooms with multiple sleeping accommodations?

At least this bed was larger than the last. Even tucked into the corner beneath a slanted ceiling lined with thick wooden beams, it nearly took up half the room. The rest was dedicated to a small table—for two, of course—and a stone fireplace, already lit. Shockingly, there was a small bathing chamber connected, likely only big enough for necessities.

A window sat at the foot of the bed, moonlight reflecting off Lumin Lake far in the distance and casting a white sheen over soft sheets that were too damn alluring for this. They drew visions of tan skin bathed in midnight and a laugh like starlight.

The door snicked shut behind me. The air in the room tightened and dragged me from those thoughts.

"I'll sleep on the floor," I grumbled, dumping my pack at the end of the bed and removing my sleeping mat. The fire in the grate ensured the room was warm enough that I wouldn't need many blankets, despite the chill beating against the window.

I could light our extra mystlight lamps if needed, but it seemed the magic supply in Castani wasn't abundant. Typical of these smaller villages.

Unfurling the mat, I added, "We'll leave early and head west to the temple network now that we're out of the mountains." There was a cluster of eleven scholarly sites in the center of the territory that Vale was hopeful would hold answers for her thanks to their strong magical concentration.

"Cypherion..."

Spirits, my name on those damn lips. And the breathy way it came out.

"It's fine," I snapped, ignoring the tingles spreading along my spine.

Same as I did every time this argument arose. For the first week and a half of the journey, we'd camped beneath the stars in utter silence. Vale had tried to break each moment of quiet. With stories across mystlight lanterns as we cut north through the mountains or conversation about the territory we descended into, she'd tried to break my walls.

Didn't she break them long ago?

I shook the thought off and continued discarding my cloak and assortment of weapons, ignoring the soft sounds of Vale doing the same as she disappeared into the attached bathing chamber.

The click of the door had me releasing a tight breath.

I was dutiful, because traveling with Vale to Starsearcher Territory to solve whatever was blocking her readings—and decipher if it was tangled in the Angelcurse—was the job assigned to me as Second to the Revered. I needed to make sure she slept, ate, and survived, so I always found a reason not to share a bed and rose before the sun to retrieve breakfast and ready the horses.

Not because I couldn't stand seeing those wide green eyes first thing in the morning—eyes full of innocence and wistful vulnerability.

Certainly not because of that.

The short days of winter made this journey achingly long, though, and I was more worried with each day that passed.

What was happening in the southern mountains? Ophelia had written in little detail to avoid private information being leaked. Kakias was dead, and something about the spirit of the Engrossian Angel Bant. My muscles tightened at the thought.

The fae had called in a bargain with Ophelia, and they were set to meet the bloodthirsty queen sometime soon—apparently the ruler of Vercuella had not set a specific time.

From the curt tone of her letters, Ophelia was thrilled about that.

Regardless, this war was over—for now. My friends had fought while I was traipsing through mountains and jungles.

My fingers curled on the buckles of my leathers as I undid them. I should have been there.

You could have rejected this mission, I argued with myself as I removed the top layers and tunic and sat before the fire, feet riskily close to the grate. The warmth heated the nerves I'd tried to numb into a stoic monotony these past few weeks. They all threatened to unravel more and more each day.

"I need your help."

"I'll do whatever I can."

Sighing, I braced my elbows on my knees and my face in my hands. Breathed in and out slowly to steady myself, to forget those two sentences that haunted me and the flashes of memory that came with them. To focus on my assignment instead.

Ophelia had been threatening to pull rank to send me here; it was clear in her tone, and I'd refused at first.

A part of me, though...

Involuntarily, my gaze drifted toward the bathing chamber.

A brutally defensive and bordering on hostilely possessive part did not want anyone else being Vale's guard.

It should be me with her.

The door to the bathing room swung open, and she caught me staring like a longing fool. I stifled my reflexive groan just in time.

I'd thought the Spirits were cruel to me before?

Vale stepped into the room and froze, wearing nothing more than a slip of silk for a nightgown, her hair dripping across her shoulders and pinning the fabric to her body. Her eyes landed on me, widening at the realization that I was half naked, and a flush crept across her skin, a comb tumbling from her hand.

The Spirits were fucking dead to me.

She bent to pick up her comb, flashing more of those lithe legs. One strap dipped down, and her silver tattoo glinted on her shoulder.

Angels, what poor fucker had I been in another life to deserve this? She was torture, every inch of her a punishment designed specifically for me—a torture my entire body was *too* aware of.

"I have to go and"—I shot up from the ground and reached for the tunic I'd just removed—"check on the food."

Her bottom lip caught between her teeth, and dammit, this was an act I could write by now. The sequence of reactions she had when I shoved her away. Eyes wide, lip caught, gaze searching through the hurt, wondering if she should say something and ultimately deciding not to. Then, the slightest drop of her shoulders and lift of her chin, and she'd say—

"As you must."

Those three words—her response nearly every time I'd avoided her. I couldn't figure out why she always chose the exact same sentence, the replicated tone.

As I pulled my tunic back over my head and stuffed my feet into my boots, grabbing parchment and Mystique ink from my bag, I told myself to stop fucking picking her words apart. To stop caring.

It only led to more pain.

Chapter Two
Vale

I kept my chin high until the door closed behind him.

Until the creaking of the staircase was no longer audible through the thin walls.

Until I could breathe around the heavy weight on my chest and the stinging in the back of my eyes.

But his bergamot and sage scent crowded the air, and the avoidance ripped at my heart.

It hurt, the way he looked at me now. Or the way he didn't, I should say. Like the wishes on stars and secrets exchanged in the quiet mountain nights meant nothing. Like each kiss had been me digging out the earth for his own grave. That's what he believed. But every word I'd said to him, every confession and comfort, had been true.

Just because I'd been lying for Titus did not mean I let those things bleed into whatever had dawned between us.

I had to lie. I had no choice. Titus was my...well, I didn't know what he actually was. I wasn't sure I ever *had* known.

As Starsearchers, we did not just read fate. We were *tied* to the Fates—a distinct difference most other clans did not understand. There'd once been twelve Fates, but one had died a brutal, betrayed death when only the gods spun tales in the skies.

As children, we learned of the eleven remaining, but it wasn't until we grew in our searching practice that we were drawn to one over the others. Sometimes, rarely, more than one. And Titus had me swear I would never reveal my truth about the Fates.

No matter how badly I wanted to.

No matter how much that hurting pair of blue eyes pierced my soul each time I caught them looking to me for an explanation. For some way to make my secrets make sense.

Alone in the room, I rubbed a hand against my sternum. My entire chest was tight. Not just from Cypherion's avoidance, but from the pressure of my magic begging to be released. I'd never stifled it.

I *hated* stifling it.

Incense snuck beneath the crack in the door. Not enough to consume me, but enough that, maybe, I could try to read something. Tentatively, I closed my eyes and grasped for the readings sitting beneath the surface of my skin.

Reaching into my magic was like dipping a toe in a pool of starlight. But instead of the ripples cascading outward, they shot into me. The voices of the Fates crowded my mind, blurred so I couldn't read a word they said.

Flashes of white fire, like the tails of falling stars, burned behind my eyelids, and in them, I could barely make out muddled fortunes. They should have been painted there, clear as the dawn. The voices shouldn't have been layered but guiding.

My limbs shook, darkness consuming the edges of my session. It was heavy, like the darkness I'd once seen surrounding Ophelia. Opening its maw, it tried to swallow me down.

With the force of the Fates, I wrenched myself from the reading and stuffed it all back down.

Panting, I braced a hand on the window. That reading of

Ophelia—the one that showed darkness converging on Gallantia—was one of the last true readings I'd done when I first arrived in Damenal. Titus had claimed it as his own and instructed me not to conduct any more sessions while with the Mystiques.

I'd still tried when requested, but I'd burned herbs that would counteract any true reading.

And by the time I was truly attempting to read again—after the Battle of Damenal when my secrets were exposed—nothing worked correctly. My position with the Mystiques had been shattered, like a delicate pane of glass.

And Cypherion did not want to discuss any of it. No explanations, no excuses. I curled my fingers against the glass and breathed in deeply—just once. Then I let it go, as I let *him* go every time he turned his back on me these past few months.

Despite the way it sliced my heart right down the center, I let him go.

I *had* to let him go.

Releasing a breath, I looked out the window. Lumin Lake stared at me like a sheet of deep blue stained glass, roughly half a day's journey away.

The temple containing all my earliest memories stood proudly on the cliff on the southeast side. Barely visible from here, sure, but I knew it loomed. As if it was a fate I couldn't escape no matter how hard I tried.

Those pillars formed some contrived combination of safety and shackles. The two ideas melted together in my head, as they did every time I tried to pry them apart.

What was the truth?

How was I supposed to feel?

My chest ached.

The window was cold beneath my palm, but I let the sting settle in as the memories did. Diving in the lake during those early summers and playing on balconies swarmed by incense as the sun faded into stars. Stories and lessons and training to be the defense of the secrets buried within our sacred spaces. Slaps on flesh and loud, assuming remarks—

I inhaled sharply, eyes squeezing shut and hand trembling against the glass.

Not those memories. *You were rescued from those.* Something within me tugged at the reminder.

I had few earlier memories than life at the Lumin temple. Fuzzy things that poked into dreams every now and then.

Bursts of laughter and bare feet on cobblestones, soft jungle moss between my toes and sunlight peeking through ferns. The earliest years of life that no one truly remembered in detail, mainly drowned by the polished marble floors and harsh instructors that came later.

I had more recent recollections, too, but the thought of touching them had my pulse racing.

I brushed them all away, one by one, and turned my back on the view of the temple. The good and the bad. Tucked it all into that dusty, worn box in my mind where the lid was peeling back at the edges from constant opening and closing.

Especially in recent months.

I'd hidden it away for good once I received the tattoo on my shoulder...until someone convinced me to open it up, one truth at a time.

It hadn't been enough, though, I thought as I perched on the bed.

Curling my feet beneath me, I leaned against the pillows, full and feathered, despite the ramshackle state of the inn. I toyed with the corner of the soft sheets, my gaze automatically swinging between the door and the window every few seconds like I was some weak-minded, simpering young girl, desperate for a hint of acceptance.

I wasn't.

I couldn't be.

If I was, being back here would surely destroy me. I'd withstood barred cages my entire life, had learned what they were comprised of. I could summon their familiar iron-strength and forge it within myself.

My gaze caught on that cursed sleeping mat unrolled before the fire.

I'll take the floor, he had said. Cypherion Kastroff was always such a stars-damned gentleman. I hated it.

No, that was a lie.

I *wanted* to hate it. But I'd seen the other side of him. The one I suspected he rarely let anyone see. The one that drove him to fighting rings after the Battle of Damenal and kissed like he wanted to consume you. It was possessive and passionate and— Spirits, heat gathered in my core at just the memory of it.

I'll take the floor.

"Valyrie's tits!" I cursed, throwing the pillow across the room. It knocked a statue carved of blue stone from the mantle, sending it shattering to the floor. I didn't bother to pick up the pieces.

If I could go back to those long nights in Damenal when we'd begun cracking open wounds, to the eve of Daminius, when a fear I'd never seen in Cypherion turned those blue eyes gray, I would.

"I need your help."

"I'll do whatever I can."

Perhaps I could have found a way to help while still keeping Titus's secrets.

Titus...his name crawled along my skin.

A captor, a pseudo-father.

A teacher, an iron fist.

A savior, a friend.

No matter how much it fogged my brain, he was all of those things.

But his decrees over my readings had torn apart the safe haven I built for myself within the arms of Cypherion Kastroff, and despite all the chancellor had done for me, resentment burned through me at that fact.

And Titus's silence now only confused my thoughts more.

Reflexively, my fingers drifted across that tattoo on my shoulder. The brand I'd been given as a child to mark me as property of Lumin Temple. A ring of eleven stars inked over in glittering silver when I was taken in by Titus. A burn made beautiful.

I didn't have the answers for how I should feel toward the man, but losing Cypherion had deepened the hole the chancellor's actions dug within me.

Perhaps it wasn't too late, though.

Cypherion had avoided me as much as possible on this journey, but he was *here*. And that meant something, even if honor was forcing him into it.

We needed answers if I was truly going to prove my alliance with the Mystiques and read anything of the Angelcurse and the darkness I'd once seen surrounding the Revered.

He is only here on orders, I reminded myself. *And to get the answers his friends need.* Because he loved them fiercer than most loved in their entire lives.

But Cypherion had been there each time my readings malfunctioned. When I woke in the Labyrinth in Mindshaper Territory, dazed and weak, he was the face looming above me. His was the voice whispering it was all right.

He has barely spoken to me or looked at me since.

I dropped my head into my hands. I kept coming back to Cypherion's actions rather than his lack of words. The gentle—reluctant—care he sometimes showed.

Rising from the bed, I drifted back toward the window. Placed my palm against the glass, blocking the temple.

And I swore, if there was a part of Cypherion Kastroff that still cared for me, a part not completely scorned by my lies, I would find it.

And I would earn his heart back, even if only as a friend.

Be meek, be quiet, be observant, Titus had instructed me when we first went to Damenal. I was done with it all. I was blessed by the Fates, and I would let that starlight burn through me.

Chapter Three
Cypherion

"Anything else?" the barkeep asked, a different one than the man with large ears. This one's voice was soft, her eyes dark as coal and hair somehow darker.

"Two ales, please."

She nodded, wandering down the bar to grab the drinks. I fished the coins from my pocket and left them for her.

Pulling a stool out, I nearly fell into the seat and leaned on the corner between the bar top and wall, head thudding back against the wood and eyes closing. I needed to calm myself down, regain some semblance of control.

There was a dull *thunk* and the jingling of the coins I'd dumped on the bar.

"Thank you," I said without opening my eyes.

"Food will be out shortly," she answered, and her steps faded into the chatter through the dining room.

With Vale upstairs and away from the watchful crowd, I was able to settle down. Able to tune out the obnoxious conversation of the men bordering on obscenely intoxicated. I was glad I'd come to get food rather than Vale.

And there she is, consuming my thoughts again.

Grumbling, I took a swig of ale. It was light with a hint of orange, one I hadn't tried before. Tolek would probably like it, but I preferred something more bitter. Stronger.

At least I had two.

Trying to distract myself, I pulled out a piece of parchment and my well of Mystique ink. Not that this was any more pleasant than the Starsearcher upstairs, but at least writing these letters was a routine I could walk through each day to make it feel like I was doing something useful. My friends liked to tease my orderly habits, but a list of tasks kept me focused. And focus meant I was earning something. Albeit, as I scrawled the letter, I couldn't quite say *what* I was earning.

Perhaps the title of doting son. Though, would one who qualified as "doting" truly have left?

As I folded the slip of paper and sent it off over the nearest mystlight, to a city hundreds of miles away, I tried not to picture the cold, empty house, cruel winter air streaking through cracks between the molding. Elbows braced on the bar, I scrubbed my hand over my face.

At the table behind me, someone complained, "No, Carthern, we can't lose any more money!"

"I hear there's a big beast of a warrior fighting these days," a man muttered, trying to keep his voice down, but my attention was caught by that one word. *Fighting*. "He just returned from the battles down south. Quiet and broody, spoiling every night. Always wins."

"If he always wins, then we won't get much coin betting on him."

"That's where you're not listening to my plan, Allisman. We bet *against* him."

My knuckles burned with memories of fights splitting them open. Stinging, blood dripping slow and warm across the cracked skin. I flexed my hands, that familiar itch starting in the tips of my fingers and traveling all along my body, longing for a fight. To check off another title earned.

Needing it.

I bit back the urge. I had a job here, one that would be jeopardized by giving into impulsive desires.

"Nah, you haven't thought that through," Allisman, dismissed. "People are rarely betting coin nowadays."

"They're trading something better." There was a hungry tone to Carthern's ambition now, bordering on greedy. My fingers curled around the edge of the counter. The barkeep dropped our food before me, but I barely looked at the tray. "They're trading *fates*."

The wooden legs of my stool scraped against the floor as I shot up, spinning to crowd their table.

"Where are they?" I ground out, fingers flexing at my sides. Spirits, I wished I still wore my blades. Not only was I exposed without them, but warriors were much more willing to negotiate with a glint of steel reflecting in their stare.

"Where are what?" Carthern echoed. He was gaunt, but his eyes shone.

"The fighting rings you're talking about." I braced my hands on the table, leaning further into their space. Not enough to be entirely overbearing, just a shadow of intimidation. "Where are they?"

I could go tonight. Vale was safe upstairs. She wouldn't miss me, and if I won and could earn a piece of information about the Starsearchers' celestial readings without having to expose her secrets—

"Lumin."

Angel's fucking luck. Half a day away.

I pushed back upright, crossing my arms. "Those are the closest?"

"Those are the ones worth entering if you want something valuable," Carthern answered. The other man—who I guessed was his brother based on their similar hazel eyes, sloping noses, and firm brows—didn't comment. He only assessed me, lips pursed.

Something valuable. Not only was it all I was interested in, it was all I would risk calling attention to ourselves for.

But Lumin was far. And Vale—

"When I was four, I was taken from my family by the City Council. I was raised at the Lumin Temple until Titus found me —a prisoner, in a sense." A cracked voice and my hand on her chin pulling her attention back to me as horrors spilled from her lips. Horrors that were only half the nightmare. The half she had words for. *"I was ripped from my home as a child"*—a huge breath—*"and indebted to the temple."*

I blinked away the memory and cleared my throat. "Where exactly?"

"Cliffs overlooking the lake," Allisman finally offered. "Just west of the temple."

He proceeded to give me clear instructions on how to enter and who to speak to. All the while I pushed away thoughts of the Starsearcher upstairs.

We were all facing things we'd rather bury. We needed answers to her current reading ailment more than we could afford to hide. We could enter the city and be quick with our business.

"Thank you for the information," I said, spinning away from the table, retrieving the tray from the bar, and slipping the ink into my pocket.

Allisman and Carthern's hushed voices followed me as I stomped back up the stairs.

～

"What did you get?" Vale asked eagerly when I returned, hastily pulling lids off plates and setting the table, as if we were a picture of domesticity. "Smells delicious." She beamed.

The expression on my face had to be confused, but it didn't give her pause. Instead, she dropped into the chair and raised her brows pointedly at the other.

This is fine, I told myself as she rambled on about the shops in Castani. This was civil.

"They're known for their goods mined from the mountains. We often imported them into Valyn by way of travelers. It's one of my favorite markets." She barely flinched when she mentioned the capital, but I caught it. A subtle twist of her lips before she pulled together whatever act she was conducting. "I love the jewelry forged here."

As she spoke of the different metals and the pieces she once owned, ease slipped over her frame.

I said, genuinely sad, "It's a shame we won't see it."

Vale froze.

I froze.

That was the first sentence I'd offered freely on this entire journey. The first that wasn't an answer to her questions or an instruction, but a conversation. It had simply slipped out. I ran my hand through my hair and dropped my chin.

After a lengthy silence, Vale said. "You wrote to her."

My head snapped up, and those wide eyes that were my utter weakness were trained on the ink I hadn't realized stained my hands. Her stare pierced right through me until I had no control over my thoughts and wanted to pour every word on the table between us.

Tearing my gaze from her and pushing the meat across my plate, I said, "As always."

"And she hasn't—"

"No." My fingers tightened around my fork.

I never missed a day. Never received an answer from her hand, but sent them anyway, so she knew I hadn't abandoned her as *he* had.

Spirits, it twisted something inside my chest that Vale knew this about me. It burned in anguish, a knot of longing and regret that choked my throat and marred the civil ease we'd adopted tonight. What was worse, though, was the comfort Vale's voice worked against that knot, trying to undo it.

Ever since I'd first divulged this piece of myself, she'd done that.

"Every day since we left," I said, folding the paper and letting the ink take it away. My stare lingered where it disappeared. "Tolek stole ink from his father's reserves that night we packed up, and I've sent one letter to my mother every day."

"That's sweet of you," Vale said, and surprise had me turning toward her. The low mystlight outlined her profile, highlighting the softness of her smile and the compassion in her eyes.

She'd sought me out in my suite tonight, and I wasn't sure why. I thought perhaps she was lonely—who wouldn't be after being forced to move to a strange city, in a different territory, spur of the moment, only two weeks prior?

"I don't do it for that reason," I admitted.

Vale tilted her head, but didn't push. She did, however, perch on the corner of my desk, planting herself to stay, and the casualness of that action ticked at something inside my chest. It was an ease Tolek offered Ophelia. A gentle but wordless reassurance of, if you want to talk, I'll listen, *but without any* pressure.

"My mother is sick," I explained, swallowing and crossing the office. I fell into the worn leather chair behind my desk and toyed with a loose string in the seam. "She has been since I was little. Something in her mind, I don't know what. She doesn't see healers, but it's been over a decade of catatonic stares."

"And you've cared for her since you were a boy." There was something in her eyes I couldn't quite place.

"It's always been me. My father has never been around, so I've been it for her." I fought to keep the bitterness from my tone. "We were close when I was young. We moved around a lot until we settled in Palerman, but she was already gone by then. I wanted to start training—wanted...friends—so I enrolled myself in lessons. Met Tolek, Malakai, and Ophelia on my first day, and we never moved again."

Vale observed me for a long moment. I slammed up my

guarded expression, but she seemed to dig past it. Discomfort beat against my bones.

"Your mother hasn't answered your letters." She didn't ask questions, I realized. Vale somehow knew.

Maybe it was a Starsearcher trait, something devised from reading futures, but Vale was someone I instinctually trusted. And my instincts rarely led me astray. So, I pried open wounds and explained things I rarely shared.

I shook my head. "I write to the neighbors, too. One letter per week, a few families on a rotation. They know I'm residing in the mountains now and have promised to ensure she has food and is taken care of. It's all I hear of her."

It was the only way I could stay in Damenal. The only way I could assuage a sliver of the guilt I waded through upon leaving her.

That emotion in Vale's eyes softened further, and I finally placed it: admiration. I didn't deserve it, not for doing what anyone should do.

"Why won't we see the market?" Vale asked.

Ripping myself back from that memory, I cleared my throat. "Change of plans for tomorrow." I cleared my throat again, my voice stubbornly rough. "We have to leave early. Head toward Lumin."

Vale stiffened. "Why Lumin?"

I chewed my words carefully. "I overheard men downstairs talking about fighting rings." Her brows shot up, but I explained what they'd said and finished with, "They say Starsearchers are now betting readings rather than coin."

"I can't—"

"I'm not asking you to read," I promised. My knuckles went white from my grip on my fork at the thought. "I'm going to fight."

Vale studied me for a moment. Then—

"No," she demanded, and this time my brows rose. "I've heard about the rings in Lumin. They've always been ruthless—

dangerous. I'm sure they've only gotten worse since the war." She shook her head, as if convincing herself further. "No."

Her resolute refusal pried at something in my chest, unsettled and raw. "Too bad," I said. "You don't get to decide where and when I fight."

"Don't be so—"

"So what?" I cut her off. For a moment, we glared at each other in silence, both dropping our forks. I leaned forward. "In case you forgot, I do this often. I'm capable of beating whoever this man is, and we'll be one step closer to figuring out this mess and going home."

Her jaw ground at my choice of words. Which part exactly had done it? Was it the mention of home, since she hadn't seen hers recently?

That was the point, though. If she wanted to return to her precious Titus, we needed to finish this. To figure out why her visions were faulty and how they were tied to the Angel emblems, given that she fainted when trying to read around them.

If we wanted an end to not only this assignment, but this entire mess, we had to go to Lumin.

Then, Vale could leave like she'd always intended.

Her silence after an actual conversation tugged at my weak heart, but I shoved it off. My emotions could stay out of this.

"Fine," Vale finally conceded. "I suppose it's good I spent time around Tolek."

"Why?" I asked, eyes narrowing.

"Because I've learned how to gamble well enough that I should be able to win some information before you're beaten to death in the ring."

I couldn't help the slight quirk of my lips. "Oh, Stargirl, don't you know I never lose a fight?"

It wasn't until her eyes widened that I realized I hadn't called her Stargirl since Daminius.

Chapter Four
Cypherion

"We can't leave yet," Vale said the next morning as I strapped my scythe to my back.

"What do you mean?" I asked. My eyelids were heavy, barely having slept on that mat. She'd tried to get me to take the bed.

I'd refused.

Vale waved a hand at me, then across her own body, clad in Mystique leathers. Spirits, I'd been trying to ignore the way they hugged every one of her curves for weeks. Months, truly. Ever since we left Damenal. It was tempting, even more so knowing how her skin felt beneath them.

"We can't go to Lumin like this," Vale stated matter-of-factly.

"You suggest we *don't* wear our leathers?" The idea made my skin itch.

"We want to blend in, correct?" Vale's fingers twisted together, the thin silver ring she wore sliding around. She used to have more—adorning every finger. Now, it was just the one she refused to part with, tarnished with age.

I groaned. "What do you suggest?"

Damien had been fucking testing me this entire journey. My self-control, my dedication, my will.

They all suffered as Vale stepped out from behind the partition in the clothing shop on Castani's market street.

Tan legs slipped between the slits in her flowing skirt, a thin band of skin visible just around her waist above the sage-green material. I could sink my teeth into every inch of her—

Get it together, Kastroff.

"You can't wear that," I said.

She spun toward me with her brows raised. "I don't allow men to tell me what I can and cannot wear, Cypherion."

"Spirits," I grumbled. "I didn't mean it like that." If being friends with Ophelia and Santorina taught me anything, it was that women were free to do what they liked with their bodies. "I only meant that it's winter, and you'll freeze as we travel the jungle between here and Lumin."

The top she wore was nothing more than a thin, woven material. Granted, the sleeves were long and cascaded past her hands. But it sat off her shoulders and barely reached the bottom of her ribs.

"Leathers are a better option," I said, shifting in my seat to hide the obvious reaction of my body to her outfit.

"Mystique leathers will not blend in. Trust me." Vale turned back to the glass, not meeting my eyes again. She ran her hands over the skirt, a new set of shining silver rings adorning each of her fingers, that tarnished one now appearing dull. "And besides, I'm much more comfortable in this. I'll have other layers to defend from the cold."

I almost argued. It was illogical, but the other shelves in the shop *were* lined with boots and cloaks that appeared warm. And there was a bead of vulnerability buried beneath her words. *I am much more comfortable in this.* A defense against entering a place that haunted her.

Beside me, my sword and scythe sat with a smaller silver sword she'd gotten from Ophelia, the handle carved with a fancy guard. That wasn't the type of defense she sought, though.

Grumbling, I pushed to my feet and tried to hide the fact that my cock was stiff within my leathers. "What do I need to wear, then?"

As we purchased the items, I swiped up a deep-blue velvet cloak for Vale. It was lined with a thick, expensive fabric, silver woven through, so when the light hit it just right, it shimmered like the night sky.

Chapter Five
Vale

"I love the skirts you wear," Cypherion told me, his hands drifting over the chiffon falling around my thighs as I perched on the railing of his balcony. Damenal unspooled across the mountains below.

"Why is that?" I asked with a teasing tilt of my head.

I expected a crude joke. Something about slipping his hands beneath them so easily as he had for the first time last night, which I would have agreed with, but it wasn't what he said.

"They suit you," he said with a shrug. "You'd look devastating in Mystique leathers, but something about the skirts embodies your spirit. They feel free, like you."

After nearly a month in Damenal, I was learning how insightful Cypherion was. In the hours we'd spent training and touring the city, he'd shared a number of musings that made me think in turn. Things about life and our purpose, questions about the Fates and how Starsearcher magic worked.

Nearly every time, his words were something slightly different than what I expected. It made me hungry for whatever he would say next. To be near him was to think, to grow, to see the world in a series of questions and steps and causes—and I was becoming *dangerously entangled in how those truths made me feel about this Mystique Warrior.*

Especially after how he'd kissed me last night. His hands in my hair, body pinning mine against the wall in my bedchamber, somehow sweet and dominating all at once.

This time, though, what he'd said was not entirely correct. Nor did it make me think as I hoped. Instead, a chill wormed along my spine.

"I'm not free." My voice was small. "Not in the slightest."

"What do you mean?" His brows pulled together as he took a step closer, protective and confused all at once, and I almost told him. Almost let slip how being here in Damenal—being here and not in Valyn, being here breathing fresh mountain air without eyes burrowing into my back and beckoning my sessions—was the freest I'd ever felt, and still chains remained around my wrists.

Not literally—that hadn't happened since I was young.

But I could feel them.

And I couldn't tell him.

"Are any of us truly free?" I joked, but it didn't work. Cypherion kept searching my gaze.

So, I found what I was able to share and told him of that wretched day. "I was born in a small town near Lumin Lake. Just along the southern shores, not too far from the mountains." I could see the cottage as I spoke, hear the echoes of the family's voices I barely remembered. "When I was four, I was taken from my family by the City Council. I was raised at Lumin Temple until Titus found me—a prisoner, in a sense."

I couldn't find it in me to speak of the rest of it right now. Of what happened during those years. The brand on my shoulder flamed.

Cypherion's hand gently nudged my chin. I hadn't realized I'd dropped my gaze. Or that I was nearly crying.

"I was ripped from my home"—I took a huge breath—"and indebted to the temple."

And while Titus had rescued me, being here in Damenal was the first time I'd felt free. I didn't understand what that meant.

Cypherion's arms folded around me as I slowly unraveled more pieces of the story.

"Why, though?" he asked when we both grew quiet, my head resting on his chest as he stood between my legs, his hand gently stroking my back.

"Magic." I shrugged. The words were on the tip of my tongue. To explain it all to him. Instead, I said, "People fear power they don't understand. Instead of learning it, they seek to control it."

I didn't offer up any more. I couldn't, and he understood.

Still, as we watched the stars and whispered promises to them from our broken childhood selves, all I could imagine was a temple overlooking a lake, and the secrets lurking beneath the stone.

~

Cypherion barely looked at me the entire ride to Lumin. If I hadn't been so preoccupied repairing the pieces of myself this city had shattered nearly two decades ago, I may have minded.

My resolve to crack his icy exterior slipped a bit more with each step, but I clung to it tighter than the reins of the dappled gray warrior horse beneath me, Marage.

The cloak Cypherion had given me was soft against my skin, a reminder of the gentle side of him I wanted to win back. It slid over Marage's hide as she ambled along the path, and each time the deep blues caught the light peeking through the high branches, Cypherion's eyes flashed through my mind, the precise shade of his intent stare I'd often been on the receiving end of.

We were traveling through the jungle rather than the mountains. Damenal and the surrounding peaks ignited a sense of freedom in me, but the trees stretching to the heavens were branches of my soul sprouted in the soil.

Each frond carving our path and vine tangled overhead nourished those pieces of myself. They rooted me to the magic of the earth, calling out to my own wary gifts, and that was the familiarity I needed if I was going to survive this.

The jungle cats, the primates, even the snakes and buzzing insects...The monotony of them all soothed a bit of the lost thread my sessions had torn up within me. I burrowed into that comfort, trying to chase off the worry of what waited.

"How long did you live there again?" Cypherion finally asked. The deep tone of his voice nearly shocked me from the saddle, and I clenched my legs tighter against my mare to stay seated. He didn't specify where, and the consideration in that choice was so cautious, attentive to the details I'd given him months ago that made it clear it was difficult to speak of this city.

"Only about four years," I answered without thinking. And immediately after saying it, memories of those days came pouring back. Every anguished one, every star-blessed one. All through the eyes of a child who didn't know any better, now through the eyes of an adult who was still trying to figure them out.

"Four years," Cypherion mused. His horse was behind mine, but without turning, I could picture his thoughtful expression. The determined set of his jaw. Why was he suddenly making conversation? "Tell me something good. Something you liked about living there."

Something I liked? I'd spent so much time shrouding my memories of Lumin after I went to live with Titus. So many long nights convincing myself those years—the events I'd endured before moving to the capital—had been nothing more than nightmares.

But something good... There were a few moments that had

not become horrors. A few that were dazed dreams of the sweetest sun-kissed memories.

"The trees have the best fruit. It bursts on your tongue, and the colors are so rich."

"What were your favorites?" he prompted, voice melting into the hum of the jungle. Though it was winter, the trees held a warmth that his presence tangled with, wrapping around me.

"Blood oranges." And the words tumbled from me without my control. "Their juice is sweet with a hint of tart. There was one tree that hung over the lake right outside my balcony. I would climb on the railing, though I was told not to—Spirits, my tutor told me not to each day. I was given extra studies to try to discourage me when I was caught. Had to write the histories of the Fates repeatedly, but it only became a challenge, then. They didn't understand that I always enjoyed lessons."

And they didn't *punish* us for trivial childhood games. Only for failures in our magic.

"Because your power is important to you," Cypherion interjected quietly. Like that statement was repairing pieces of me that he'd jumbled up.

"It is," I agreed. That importance was why I was going back to Lumin at all. If I could sew up the holes in my magic, it would be worth it. "So, the chores didn't deter me."

I flashed Cypherion a smile over my shoulder, finding his eyes trained on me, blues burning like the heart of a fire. The horses continued through the jungle as our stares caught, and I said, "When I was first assigned my room, I couldn't reach the tree, no matter how hard I tried." Though I had been branded, we were each given a room as students. Fooled into thinking we were cherished guests. "By the time I was seven, though—my last summer there—I was able to stand on the railing, on my toes, and stretch so my fingertips brushed the branches. I only fell in the water once, and H—"

I cleared my throat and faced forward, hands tightening on the reins as I took a shaking breath.

"My friend laughed about it for weeks."

Cypherion wanted to ask; I knew him well enough to know he was trying to reassemble my past to make sense of me now. The questions burned into my spine as his eyes stayed locked there.

"When I moved to Palerman," he began, and I froze, "I didn't know what to make of those kinds of friendships."

I nearly balked at him offering up a piece of himself, something he hadn't done in months, but I didn't want to scare him into silence again. So, I kept my eyes on the gaps in the trees, the lake sparkling crystal blue in the distance, and I remained the judgment-free, silently attentive audience he needed.

"They—Tolek and Malakai, Ophelia and Santorina—basically forced their company on me. I waited for them to stop." He'd told me a bit about those early days in Palerman when he was twelve, but mainly about his mother. Cypherion's friends were...well, they were something even more special to him. Something that brought about a weakness he didn't often show.

I'd seen it once.

"They didn't give up," he continued, a quiet laugh. "I shouldn't be surprised. They dragged me into their games, trainings, and formal dinners practically the first day we met. I think they recognized something in me that I didn't even see. Something I still don't know how to name."

"It's almost like they always knew what you were destined for."

Cypherion grunted in response.

I pressed on. "I mean it. You were destined to be a part of their group. It's clear to anyone who sees you all."

"A part of a group, maybe," he said.

And I corrected, "A leader among the great warriors of our generation."

Another grunt. He was tending toward the abrasive quiet

he'd adopted for the first few weeks of our journey, and already I missed the sound of his voice.

"You don't believe in destiny? The Fates?" I asked. There. A question he must answer.

"It's not that," Cypherion said.

"Then, what?"

"I don't believe in a title being *my* fate, no."

"I've never known you to be so wrong, Cypherion Kastroff." When I used his full name, something like lightning buzzed between us.

He might have felt it, too, because his voice was gravelly as he said, "I haven't earned it. The title."

Spirits, he was so wrong.

"One day, you'll see that you have" was all I said, because he'd given me more conversation than he had in weeks, and I was afraid of forcing him away again so soon.

Cypherion cleared his throat. "The memories I have from those early years in Palerman, that security from when my friends took me in, really helps with"—he paused; I peeked over my shoulder, and he waved a hand around the jungle—"all of this we're facing."

My heart tugged, and elation swirled through me, knowing he'd retained that sort of love and acceptance in his life. But it combined with sadness that I hadn't. And a bit of fear that we were heading right back into all of those memories, rocking the unsteady foundation of myself.

"That's beautiful," I said quietly. "You're lucky to have them."

I wasn't sure what part of my comment did it, but Cypherion's shields snapped back up so quickly, I practically heard the metal doors of his mind slam.

"We're almost there," he said. "We'll eat, and I'll head out soon, but you can remain hidden if you'd like."

Hidden? I may be afraid, but I would not cower.

"I'll be fine," I said, lifting my chin though my form fought to crumble.

Cypherion opened his mouth to argue but snapped it shut again. Swallowed. "Right. You'll take care of yourself. I'll just... do what I have to."

Shocked, I nearly pulled my horse to a stop to ask what he meant, but spires pierced the azure sky up ahead, and my remaining strength was punctured by each gleaming point.

So I whispered, "As you must."

As the trees broke, and Lumin came into view below vine-covered cliffs, Cypherion took the lead on the path, allowing me a moment of reprieve. A moment to breathe in a city I hadn't seen in sixteen years and exhale all the poison it left in my veins.

And though neither of us said anything, I followed as he led us the long way around the city toward the location of the fighting rings, on a path that avoided the temple.

Chapter Six
Cypherion

Objectively, Lumin was a beautiful city. The lake was nestled against the mountains, the jungle surrounding it broken up by pockets of buildings that filled sloping hills down to the crystal blue water.

Various shades of pale stone comprised the city itself, homes and storefronts fitting together like puzzle pieces in slightly different hues that complemented each other. Mosaics covered the walls and greenery poured out of the jungle to tangle around pillars and homes.

But it all crawled beneath my skin.

Before I'd ever laid eyes on this city, I'd heard the pain of a young girl tied to a temple. I'd heard of the tears she'd cried at night and the marks left on her body.

Vale had painted a picture of serenity and bliss with her stories of fruit and swimming in the lakes, and that had been my goal. To give her something beautiful to remember as she entered a place she loathed.

But I couldn't see past it. As we left the inn, and I followed Vale through the city, I had a feeling she couldn't forget it either.

And I wanted to burn it all down.

"Just this way." Vale's voice was stronger than I'd anticipated. When I turned to face her, she was clear-eyed.

Guard up, Stargirl.

She waved a hand down the block, and we continued quietly. The city bustled, though. Shoppers ran down cobbled streets, bags drooping from the market as they headed home to prepare dinner. Kids screeched, releasing bouts of energy they'd likely kept bottled up during their lessons all day.

Normal life did exist in Lumin, I guessed. Despite what went on in the temple, despite what we were currently here to do. It was an unsettling reminder that everywhere, *every day* persisted around us no matter what shit we were in.

Vale turned a corner, and the next street was shadowed by a large structure, white stone glowing in the setting sun, and a mosaic dome glinting proudly with its silver spires.

"Vale, why—"

"I had to face it," she muttered. And she strode across the street with her chin high, pressing one hand to the smooth wall.

She was still for a long while, and a part of me wished I knew what was going through her head. *Don't ask, Kastroff.*

Instead, I gave her a moment of privacy, and observed the historic—horrific—Lumin Temple. With the ethereal glow of golden rays and stained glass, it was beautiful—if I didn't know what had occurred inside years ago. What might still happen at the hands of the temple masters.

The Starsearcher crest adorned the dome—a circle of eleven stars with a gap where a twelfth used to be—as it did every flag in this city.

"For the Fates," I whispered, gesturing to a pennant draping above the temple wall.

Vale's gaze swiveled toward me. "The stars are the eleven existing. The gap is the lost Fate."

The silken symbol wavered in the breeze. I studied the wall again, the stone etched with depictions of the eleven existing fates, the twelfth carved away, like a great beast's claws had gouged it out.

Dragging a hand along the rough surface, I walked a few feet and found the one I was looking for. There weren't names—the Fates' names were only given to the Starsearchers—but I recognized the rendition.

"Cruelty and Adoration," I muttered.

Vale's breath hitched. "You remember?" she asked.

I looked at her, saying firmly, "I remember everything."

"CRUELTY AND ADORATION," Vale said wistfully as we strolled through the quiet back alleys of Damenal.

My brows shot up.

"What?" She laughed, and the sound made my throat dry out.

I licked my lips. "A bit of a juxtaposition."

"All the Fates are," she explained. Her hand brushed mine as she turned to study a shop window full of precious gems, and my heart stuttered like I was thirteen years old again.

We were in one of the wealthiest parts of the city—not because I was trying to impress her, but because in the month since she'd arrived in Damenal, it was one of the few we had yet to explore. And truthfully, the silence was relaxing. The sound of her voice melodic as we wandered, a break from the strategy meetings we were in all day.

"All the Fates are counters to themselves?" I asked, studying the rings catching the setting sun in their velvet boxes. Sapphires, emeralds, rubies—even an extravagant cluster of pearls that complemented the single opal Vale always wore, the silver tarnished.

"All magic in this world and all others requires a balance, Cypherion," she explained. "The Fates are beings of magic—they are no exception."

"*So, Cruelty and Adoration is the Fate that you're aligned with?*"

Vale kept her eyes trained on the glass, nodding. "She passes me such powerful readings."

"*And they center around those two things?*"

"*Those, and many more. Always connected in one way or another.*"

"*How?*" *I asked, crossing my arms.*

"*Adoration comes in many forms.*" *Her eyes turned up to mine. "It can be love, passion, poetry." My heart raced at the intensity of her stare. "And cruelty...well, can't cruelty be a consequence of all those things, as well? They go hand in hand, a spectrum stretching between them. And every reading the Fate of Cruelty and Adoration passes to me falls along that spectrum."*

The darkness Titus read in Ophelia's future. That could have been cruelty. One we remained blind to, though Vale was trying every day to decipher what the chancellor's reading meant.

"*And these spectrums are all...various states of being?*" *I clarified.*

"*Some are. Fate of Chaos, Fate of Wrath, it goes on.*" *Vale pushed away from the glass. Taking a few steps into the alley, she drew a circle in the air. "Think of the Fates as a sphere. They orbit like true stars, three-dimensionally rotating around us at all times. And in the center, are the Starsearchers." She pretended to draw a line from the perimeter to the middle of that circle. "We conduct sessions here on Ambrisk, and they stretch out to us, burning in the wake of stars falling from the sky."*

She dropped her arms. "That's what it looks like, at least. The images I'm shown appear in the trails of starfire burning in their wake."

"*You explain it beautifully,*" *I commented. I could listen to her talk about her magic for days.*

She smiled softly, ducking her head. "It's a beautiful part of my life."

"*Come on, Stargirl,*" *I said, placing a hand at her back to guide her down the street. Her cheeks flushed at the name, and I froze.*

I'd been thinking of her that way for a bit now, like a woman who walked among the stars—who shone brighter than them—somehow falling into my life. But I hadn't meant for it to slip out.

I'd say it every chance I got if it caused that rosy blush, though.

I inclined my head back toward the palace. "Tell me more about them on the walk home."

And though the concept of the Fates was still foreign to me, it was feeling more like she might be mine.

~

"I REMEMBER EVERYTHING." My fucking words were too pining.

I cleared my throat, opening my mouth to say we had to go, but Vale spoke over me. "I remember everything, too, Cypherion."

Then, she flipped up her hood and left, the velvet cloak I'd given her swaying around her frame. And for the sake of my fucking spirit, I wouldn't admit how much I liked to see her wear it.

~

IT WASN'T hard to locate the rings given that they weren't a secret. Organized fights weren't illegal so long as all participants consented—or no one knew they hadn't. Carthern had said to look for a dark-blue flag marking the entrance and take the back stairs to the underground haven.

As we entered, my pulse raced with the familiar jeers of the crowd. With the roars of bets being called, won, and lost. It was rowdy and obnoxious and would have been entirely comfortable for me to sink into and lose myself had I not had Vale at my side.

We cut through the main bar, and no fewer than seven warriors appraised her. I fought the urge to punch their teeth out for it. Because I was her guard. That was why.

"Did you bring a weapon?" I muttered.

Quietly, Vale flashed me the triple-bladed dagger sheathed at her thigh, a Starsearcher signature throwing knife.

"Good girl." I hated that I cared.

This fighting space was smaller than the one I frequented in Damenal, but it was just as crowded. Tables and alcoves lined the circumference, booths were veiled behind sheer curtains, and a window was tucked to one side where Starsearchers dropped their bets.

The center ring was a dust floor lined by thick red ropes, sprinkles of crimson staining it. As I watched those spots fade into dirt, and a warrior was dragged from the arena, my blood heated.

I shook off the urge for the time being, focusing instead on the woman I was responsible for.

Vale was quiet when we entered, her eyes darting around the space from beneath her hood. Cataloging everything, I was certain, but she also seemed to be searching for something. As we made our way toward the betting window, she inhaled sharply, turning and heading down a path between a few tightly-packed tables.

I followed, not questioning her. There was pain I didn't understand buried within her at being here, and this was not the place to discuss it.

Not that she would even tell me. The memory of her secrets soured in the back of my throat, blurring the niceties we'd exchanged today.

"He's unstoppable," a man bragged, and I instantly knew who they were speaking of. The only opponent I wanted to fight. "He's taken down every contender the past six nights."

"I don't believe it," another argued.

"It's true!" The first one dropped his voice. "Ledger came

straight from the war. Saw some things that changed him. Now...sorry to any poor guy who stands against him."

He couldn't be that strong...could he? For once, a hint of doubt tainted my mind.

"Come on," I said stiffly to Vale, tilting my head toward the betting window and leaving those men behind.

Approaching the teller, I spoke in a low voice. "I'd like to put my name in for the next round against your current victor. Ledger."

The man appraised me. "Next fight with Ledger starts after these two are done." He nodded to the ring behind me, two scraggly warriors currently—unskillfully—trying to outlast each other. It seemed the drink swaying their steps was a bigger threat than the fight.

"Put my name in for it," I commanded.

Smirking as if he didn't believe in me, the teller ducked beneath the counter and returned with a piece of parchment. The inkwell he passed me was filled with a silver liquid. It radiated with magic, but it wasn't Mystique ink.

It likely came from the mountains, like ours did. Mined and imbued in some way. And if it was to sign a betting slip, I would put money on it being binding when one signed their name.

That was fine. I didn't intend to back out of this fight.

I reached for the parchment, but the man pulled it away at the last moment. "You can sign, but *her* signature is the one that matters."

My voice dropped into a growl as his eyes landed on Vale, and I nearly snapped the pen in half. "Why?"

The man's eyes dragged over me, snagging on the blades tucked into the vambraces at my wrist, where the mystlight illuminated a distinct Mystique sigil. *Damien's balls.*

"Should've left the foreign blades at home," he said.

Vale had convinced me to leave my scythe at the inn, but I hadn't been comfortable without *any* weapons. I should have bought triple blades, even if just for show.

"Everyone who loses is required to give a reading," he continued. "You clearly are not capable of doing that."

"And if I win?" I asked.

He scoffed. "*If* you win against Ledger, you'll hear from *her*." He gestured over his shoulder where a dark curtain was drawn, beaded chains dangling before it. "True names only. The ink will know."

Grumbling, I signed the slip of paper and slid it to Vale. Wary eyes met mine.

I dropped my voice low enough that only she would hear and swore, "You're not going to have to read. I won't let that happen."

"Cypherion," she whispered, "I'm rethinking this—"

"You're rethinking this?" I snapped, brows raised. Was she concerned for me? And why did a part of me want her to be?

"Yes, *I* am rethinking this! It involves me." Her eyes locked on the paper, my signature blatant and shining. Full first name and everything. "I can't attempt anything here."

The fear in her tone grated through my chest. I shoved that away.

She was worried about herself. Only herself, as always. Fine, but I would do what I needed to win this information and stay true to my cause here.

"I promise you won't come near a reading, Vale. No incense, nothing." She hesitated, not meeting my eyes, so I took a step closer. "I swore to protect you when I accepted this mission. I swore to see you back to Starsearcher Territory to retrieve whatever answers we could find and fix your sessions so you can aid Ophelia. I won't let that vow break in something as basic as a fighting ring."

Her brows drew together, working through something I'd said. Or something I didn't. Spirits, I didn't know. But whatever it was had a small bead of hurt widening in her eyes.

"I know these people, Cypherion. You don't."

Apparently my promises held little weight to her, because she didn't even acknowledge it.

"This is happening, Vale." My tone was harsher than usual, but desperation was sending my nerves into a riot. We didn't have time for this, and I couldn't afford the distraction.

No matter how much it twisted my gut.

"You may be a victor in Damenal, but here they won't—" Her eyes flitted around the dim room, latching onto someone or something, I didn't care. I kept my stare on her and didn't miss when she took a sharp breath, lifted her chin, and blinked a few times.

Unsettled.

Spirits, it ripped at that stirring instinct in my chest, but I fought it down, locked all the doors that it may try to escape through.

"They won't play fair," Vale said. Why did she even care?

"Good thing I won't either, Stargirl." I tapped the paper. "Sign."

She mumbled something beneath her breath, but as I started taping up my hands, she did as I said. We didn't speak as I discarded my vambraces and weapons, removing my tunic and tying back part of my hair with a leather band.

Once the bet was sealed behind the counter, I turned away, ready to storm toward the rope and shut out the jeering crowd. But Vale snatched my arm just above the tape. Skin against skin, her warmth rocked through my body.

"Be careful," she muttered, only loud enough for me to hear.

I couldn't afford that right now. Not heading into a fight that she was right about: it would not be fair. It would take everything I had to win and uphold that promise to keep her safe.

If I was going to get us both out of here with a reading that would hopefully give us answers, I had to remember that she didn't want to stay. She chose to lie, chose the chancellor who used her, over me.

So, I looked over my shoulder and met those olive eyes. Forced myself to memorize the hurt that bloomed as I growled, "Why do you care, Vale?"

I ducked beneath the rope and faced the mountain of a warrior who had spread his name across the territory. His frame was a bit larger than mine, but our height was about even. Long onyx hair was knotted at the back of his neck so opponents would not pull it, and the wrap around his hands was stained. Not replaced after each fight as a professional did, but trying to intimidate me instead.

Organizing all those details, I forgot everything else.

I shut out Vale's damaged expression and the way it panged through my chest. I shut out the mission I was here on and the worry I carried for my friends down south. I shut out my own opinions and the hurt I clung to.

And when my fist connected with Ledger's jaw for the first time, a depraved part of me sang.

CHAPTER SEVEN
VALE

You never forget the smack of fists on flesh. Not when it was a scar burned into the delicate recesses of your childhood mind. Critical, formative years lost to it.

Helpless, too young to do anything. That was how I felt again as Ledger's fist met Cypherion's cheek.

The fight had been going on for four minutes already according to the clock ticking away above the ring. Most didn't last this long even, and they weren't appearing to slow down.

Four minutes of both fighters getting in blows.

Body numb, my fingers tightened around the rope as Cypherion took another punch. His head snapped back as he stumbled. He righted himself, scanning his opponent, but not quickly enough to avoid a second hit to his ribs.

I winced, practically feeling that one myself. It was going to bruise, if not fracture.

How did he not dodge it? He had tracked that hit, watched it and tried to move but not quickly enough. His reflexes were usually faster than that.

Cypherion swung out, but Ledger moved impossibly quickly, rotating around the back of him. And Cypherion seemed disoriented.

"No, no, no," I muttered, cutting through the crowd to pace around the ring, my stomach knotting. I ignored their complaints and slurs—rowdy viewers stepping on my skirt and elbowing me—tugging my cloak tighter around me as I followed Cypherion's dizzying, dancing steps.

I wasn't in the fighting den, though. Not fully.

A part of my mind was back in the temple, watching a friend be *punished* for incoherent readings. I had rarely been hit, as my magic was stronger, but I watched. And as Cypherion barely dodged another blow, it all rushed back to me.

Marble that once shone, now smeared with blood. *Had they always been tainted?* I'd wondered in later years, when the memories woke me in the night, in a city far away from the pain.

As you must, we were to say as the punishments were doled out.

They scrubbed the floors spotless, but how clean could marble really be after that? Some stains tarnished the brightest stars.

Some broke them entirely.

Ledger ducked Cypherion's next hit and caught his wrist, swinging it behind his back, and I winced. Cypherion stifled a pained grunt, but it radiated down my bones.

He could have cried out, and the sound would have been buried beneath the crowd's shouts, but he wouldn't reveal that hint of weakness no matter how badly it hurt.

My mind was cramped with jeers. Was my vision spotting?

A streak of blood dripped down the side of Cypherion's cheek. It crawled so slowly, like a fate suspended in time, until it finally dripped over the line of his jaw and splattered to the dirt. I stumbled along the rope further, not certain where I was going, just that I needed to do something before I watched more of that crimson stain the floor.

I wanted to get on my knees and plead for him to keep fighting, to even the score, but—my vision swam again.

"Vale?" someone said behind me, and I froze. The voice was airy with disbelief, but there are some you never forget, even after more than a decade. Particularly the ones you heard screaming under those *punishments* as a child.

Stealing a breath of confidence, I searched Cypherion's form one more time—noticed where he seemed weaker than he should—then, I turned.

And though I knew to whom that voice belonged, I gasped. "Harlen?"

Angels, I'd seen him when I entered, but I convinced myself I hadn't. Why would he still be here? In this wretched city after all these years? Why hadn't he *run*?

"Vale," he breathed again.

No, no, no—I wasn't supposed to be seen.

"I thought you were in Valyn. What—how—sixteen years, Vale." His smile was so wide, it pierced my heart. My favorite smile as children; my best friend and safety in that horrid temple. "I barely recognized you when you walked in, but I was so sure." He laughed. "I think a piece of me will always know you."

"Harlen." I had to get rid of him, but I could barely think over the pressure squeezing my chest and nerves spotting my vision.

He'd grown—of course he'd grown. Straight black hair framed his face to his shoulders, and dark eyes wore years of lessons. Harlen was only a year older than me, a brother after I'd lost—

I shook away the thought. I couldn't think about her either.

I met Harlen's eager stare, but nearly flinched at all the reminders that came crashing back. A wary wall solidified around my heart and mind, built of the betrayals of my past.

A ground-shaking thud had me whirling around again, my head spinning. Cypherion was flat on his back, the warrior having swept his legs from behind. More blood streaked his face. And then Ledger stepped closer—

Planted a booted foot right on Cypherion's outstretched hand as he tried to roll away.

He didn't yell, but I did. The room was a blur, the voices screaming louder.

"Vale," Harlen said, an arm dropping around my shoulder and squeezing me to him. I squirmed from his grasp, as foreign as the snows of Mindshaper Territory.

He looked me over with hurt in his eyes, but he didn't try to touch me again. "What are you doing here?" His eyes flicked between the ring and me as Cypherion fought off Ledger and staggered back to his feet. "Who is that?"

"A friend," I forced through my dry throat. "I'm here with him. We are...working together."

It was too much. Harlen, in this place, with the echoes of flesh beating flesh. Flashes of his small form taking punches overlaid themselves on the ring.

But no, it wasn't Harlen being beat this time.

It was the warrior I cared for so deeply, so much more than a *friend*, in the ring with blood streaking his face.

They melted together now. Harlen's dark eyes and Cypherion's blue ones. Black and auburn hair—round cheeks and firm jawlines. Boyhood ruined by split knuckles. A heart wrung-out and determined in the ring.

The blood...

My vision rippled, like I was held beneath the surface of a roiling sea. My muscles were locking up. This was more than panic.

A familiar terror clawed its way up my throat.

"Harlen, is there—" My tongue was heavy, but Cypherion stumbled again, and I forced the words out. "Do people read in here?"

Harlen's brows pulled together. "Of course." He dropped his voice, then. Leaned closer. His breath fanned across my neck, my hyper-sensitive skin prickling as I fought to keep my eyes on Cypherion. "The back rooms are isolated for official readings, but they don't look too closely at what's snuck in. Especially when it's scentless."

Scentless...

I scanned the room as best I could. Some attendees stood against the back walls, relaxed and dazed, while others clung to the ropes, desperate for their bets to land.

"They're reading *now*?" My wavering stare locked on Ledger, on the glassy-eyed, rage-fueled expression. "Is *he*?"

But I did not need Harlen's subtle, confused nod to know. Understanding collected like shattered stars in my mind, ripped apart by my broken readings. It crept through me as a session tried to take over, locking my joints and stiffening my muscles.

I stumbled, hands gripping Harlen's arms as he caught me around the waist. And I was weak enough this time, I didn't pull back.

"Vale? Are you all right?" Harlen's words were mud in my ears.

Gritting my teeth, I looked over my shoulder. Cypherion's focus was not on the fight—it was on me.

Long enough that a fist struck his bruised ribs, sending him back to the floor. Hot tears snuck down my cheeks.

"Harlen," I hissed, ignoring the reluctance tugging at my mind. "Take me somewhere private."

CHAPTER EIGHT
CYPHERION

WHERE IN THE DAMNED SPIRITS WAS SHE GOING?

Ledger's fist slammed into the side of my head again, ringing through my skull.

Shit. Shouldn't have let myself get distracted.

My hand throbbed from when he crushed it, but he hadn't dug his boot in fully, so that was healing at least.

Fucking Angels, he was strong. A worthy opponent. Despite that, I kept an eye on Vale. My chest twisted as that man's arm wrapped possessively around her waist, and she leaned into him.

Where was he taking her?

Who—

A fist to my gut sent me stumbling, the rope border of the ring burning my back as I slid against it. Cheers swarmed me, hands jostling my body as I righted myself. They hadn't placed their bets on me, but it didn't matter. They just wanted a good show.

I didn't care about any of their damn gambling sheets. Only one mattered.

The one *she* signed.

As I reset my stance, I fought to keep my attention on Ledger and scan the ring at the same time.

Vale was gone. Disappeared into the mess of hungry, drunken Starsearchers. Anger poured through me at the realization, and I charged forward, landing two consecutive hits so quickly, my opponent couldn't block. A fast, distracting jab to open his defenses, followed by a solid cross that had my injured hand ringing in pain.

A simple combination—so simple he didn't expect it. It was well-placed and disorienting.

I kept up the pace while I had the advantage.

Warrior fighting rings were brutal. They had to be in order to knock a participant down long enough to declare a winner. With our quick healing, any small injury was easy to ignore. My shoulder the Starsearcher had nearly wrenched out of place was proof of that.

Thank the Spirits he didn't dislocate it entirely. *That* would have been impossible to fight through, arm useless at my side. The constant beat of pain it currently held motivated me to swing again, straight to his cheekbone.

Before he could recover, I assessed him. Saw right through those demons lying beneath the surface. Things gathered in the recent war.

I catalogued his weaknesses as I would any opponent on any battlefield. The bruise blooming across his ribs and eye swelling shut were good targets to batter before they could heal. A small smirk graced his lips despite the blood trickling from one corner.

"What are you smiling at, Starsearcher?" I growled.

Wiping the blood from his chin, Ledger said, "You're a smart fighter, I'll admit."

Then, he charged. And he was everywhere. I'd never fought someone like him. Someone who seemed to predict my movements before—

He nailed me right in the jaw.

"Oh, on Damien's fucking grave," I cursed, spitting blood to the dirt and dancing out of his reach.

Ducking his next swing, I found Ledger's stare. Glassy. Not fully dazed, but not completely focused either. One mental eye on the Fates, one on me.

Where the fuck was Vale?

"I guess you play by different rules here," I said, lunging left to dodge a hit. "Reading my moves during a fight?"

Disgraceful, but how much of what went on in any ring was truly innocent? It was just another way to prove myself.

"Is it in the air?" I asked. Making a last-minute decision, I swung out and caught his ribs again. He hadn't been able to block that one, hadn't seen it coming with the little readings he was obviously conducting to cheat these fights. Ledger hunched over sideways.

His grin told me I was correct, though.

And Vale—fuck. Memories of her readings battered my mind.

Dread made it hard to breathe, my throat dry as Vale fell too still within that cloud of incense. Angellight burned through the room, Ophelia gone to it, her blood staining those emblems, and Tolek in a panic.

A growl rumbled in my chest, and Vale toppled to the floor.

"Vale?" I whispered, dropping to my knees beside her. Her eyes rolled back, mouth slightly ajar. "Vale!"

But her body seized uncontrollably.

I'd seen her read so deeply she exhausted herself. I'd seen her completely taken by a session during the Battle of Damenal, so far gone she didn't hear the fight around her. But this...

This was something else entirely.

Santorina was on Vale's other side. "Don't try to restrain her," she instructed me, placing a cushion under the Starsearcher's head and rolling her onto her side. "Just count."

So, I began a vigil at her side—Jezebel and Tolek shouting to

Ophelia in the background—and fisted my hands against the cool tile to stop their shaking, counting the breaths.

Come on, Stargirl, *I thought, slamming my hand against the ground.* Fight those fucking Fates.

This wasn't Vale. I may have barely been able to speak to her lately, but Vale was powerful—she was formidable with her magic.

But as she finally stopped seizing, and her heartbeat slowed to a horrifying pause, I worried that the Fates might kill her.

I had to end this fight. Had to get to her before her own readings pummeled her. She might already be weak. Images of her strewn on the ground, vulnerable and alone, dragged nausea through my gut.

I didn't stop to consider how Ledger was doing it. Just focused on Vale, so she was all anyone reading my fate would see. The desperation I pretended to ignore replaced any anticipation of my next move.

Then, I charged the warrior, shoulder slamming into the bruise on his ribs and taking him to the ground.

And I evened the score.

CHAPTER NINE
VALE

Harlen guided me through a curtain into a back room lit by candlelight, my cloak falling to the floor.

My senses and mind were assaulted by cloying incense. Not the soothing herbal embrace my magic used to provide.

"No—no, not here." I staggered against a shelf, sending vials to the floor. They shattered, and more oils wafted around us. My muscles stiffened, vision swimming in a haze of the soft shades of purples and blues draped along the walls.

"What are you doing in here?" A feminine voice sliced through the air, mingling with a clinking sound I couldn't place. My knees cracked to the tile.

"Vale." Harlen cupped my cheeks, forcing my gaze up. The room was getting dimmer, and my vision spotted. All I could make out were his dark eyes, laced with worry, maybe? "Vale, I need you to tell me what's going on."

I opened my mouth but gasped as pain split my skull, a collision of stars cleaving through my head. The Fates tightened in my chest, those starlight voices yelling, yelling, *yelling*. The fiery tails their readings waited in burned through me, ready to explode.

"Lay her here," that female voice said, and I was moved, jostled quickly until there were soft pillows under my body, one bracing my cheek.

I tried to organize my thoughts.

The rings were rigged.

They placed a warrior fierce enough in the center so that no one would question when he won repeatedly, but he was using magic to predict what would happen. The regular attendees all knew it—it was clear now who was involved by the way they'd lined the back walls, relaxed with drinks in hand, not a care in the fated realm aside from waiting for their winnings.

Was there something in the drinks to stop other Starsearchers from picking up on what the fighter could read? It was possible. Illegal, but possible. Stifle their magic so they were none the wiser.

"Vale!" a voice I recognized shouted, and it was honey over my aching mind. Sweet and warm and comforting, but it took me a moment to place it beyond that bone-deep level of rightness.

"What the fuck did you do to her?" he growled.

Concern. Always concern, even when he tried to hide it. That was how I knew it was Cypherion. My warrior.

"I didn't *do* anything," Harlen argued. "She got weak and sick and asked me to bring her somewhere."

A hand brushed across my forehead; Cypherion's voice was soft now. "Stargirl," he said, and I loved that he was using that name again. "Is it the sessions? Whatever's in the air?"

I nodded, squeezing my eyes tighter. I couldn't let the reading take over. But those voices pressed against my mind again, tendrils of starfire begging to show me all its secrets. My chest was full—it was hard to draw breath.

"Give her space," Harlen started.

But Cypherion whirled on him. "Who the fuck are you anyway?"

"Me? Who are you? You're not a Starsearcher, that's for damn sure, no matter what clothes you wear."

My disguise for him was not as good as I thought. Pity.

A swarm of stars swirled behind my eyes, luring me in.

"It doesn't matter who I am," Cypherion spat, and all I could focus on was the rough tone of his voice. *He really thinks that. He truly thinks he does not matter.* My thoughts were jumbled—I was forgetting what was important right now beyond remembering that.

I blinked against my shattering vision, wanting to tell him he was wrong.

"You're right, it doesn't," Harlen spat. *No*, my mind echoed. "I'm her best friend. Or," he stuttered, "or I was."

Regret and defense twisted his words.

"Not anymore," Cypherion argued. "Make yourself useful and get her water."

That tinkling sound again. Beads. The curtain leading to the back room. That piece of understanding about where I was calmed my racing breath.

"Cypherion," I exhaled, finally stealing back control of my muscles enough to wrap my hand around his wrist. He hadn't moved from cradling my head, and I pried my eyes open to find him kneeling beside me. The shadows were too dim and the incense too thick for me to properly see his face.

"You're here?"

"I'm here." It was relief deepening his voice, tangled with fear. "I'm here, Stargirl."

Strong arms swept beneath my legs and back, and I was cradled against a warm, bare chest. It was gentler than when I'd been moved before.

"Did you win?" I forced out to distract myself from the swarm of incense again. The once-alluring scents tangled around me, coaxing me to succumb to the pressure in my chest and head.

Cypherion huffed a laugh. "I sure did, Stargirl. Promised you I would." A shiver shot down my body, uncontrollable and violent. "Fight it," he whispered. "Fight it off, Vale, and we'll get out of here. I'll get you out of here. Just stay with me."

He started to stand, but we couldn't—

"We need," I gasped. "We need the reading. You won it."

"Doesn't matter. I'll come back for it." I could practically hear the grinding of his jaw.

Summoning every bit of control I could, I forced my hand up. My fingers skated along his chest and landed on his cheek. Sticky.

Blood.

It was drying, but in the dim light, I could just make out a nasty slice above his eyebrow. Deep. He'd probably lost so much blood already. It would scar.

Wait—what had he said? *I'll come back for it.*

No. No, he couldn't leave me alone.

Cypherion's arms tightened around me, and in my weak state, shrouded by that comfort, my tongue loosened. "Don't leave me behind," I whispered.

Not as so many people had before. Not as Titus was trying to.

I couldn't see his face when he whispered, "Never."

Harlen tore back into the room, a glass of water in hand. Cypherion set me on the cushions, retrieving my cloak and wrapping me, then helped me drink some of the water. Each swallow was brutal, but the soft velvet he'd gifted me was an unrivaled warmth.

When he was certain I wasn't going to choke, he said to Harlen without looking away from me, "Thank you. My winnings. Find them."

"No need," that feminine voice returned. The beads clinked as I let my eyes slip shut again. "I can perform the session."

So, it was her. I didn't know why Harlen brought me to the

private chambers of the ring's prized Starsearcher, the one we'd gambled to win a reading from, but I didn't have the energy to question it now.

"She should not stay," the woman said.

"She stays," Cypherion commanded before I could muster up the energy. He cradled me in his lap again.

Thank Valyrie.

Settling into Cypherion's arms, I listened as Harlen left. As the Starsearcher settled her herbs and incense, as a match hissed with flame and the light shifted outside of my lids. As silence cascaded over the room with a warm rush, and I fought off the mounting pressure in my chest.

Each time burning starfire tried to steal my mind, with each shiver that racked my body, Cypherion held on. He dragged a gentle hand down my arm and watched me, counting beneath his breath. At one point, he tightened his grip, then reluctantly shifted me to the cushions beside him, like he wanted me to lay flat, just in case.

Cypherion's eyes and hands remained on me, searing and soothing all at once. The incense struck at the walls I'd formed around my mind, and indeterminable images flashed behind my eyelids.

I clung to Cypherion's hand. *Fight it*, he'd asked of me.

Fight it, like I'd told myself I'd fight for him. This was another test. Hold on to him as I wanted to cling to the future we had not had a chance to explore.

Shapeless things flashed in my mind, all cloaked in shadows. Indiscernible and ghostly. Bursts of light pushed through.

Sweat beaded on my brow.

"Hurry up," Cypherion mumbled beneath his breath.

But it was fruitless. We couldn't rush the Fates.

Finally, a huge pair of feathered wings flared behind my eyes, iridescent before a setting sun. I cried out as the reading tugged and tugged at me.

Just in time for the searcher to break from her trance.

And she said words that sank to the core of myself, cold and terrified. "The ninth floor beneath the archives holds what you seek."

Panic gripped my chest, tearing away what little resolve I held against the reading. And it took me.

Chapter Ten
Cypherion

The sky didn't seem as dark here. In Damenal, the mountains sometimes swallowed up the light, and the stars peppered a black sheet. But here, the space between them seemed to melt into their glow. Deep pockets of navy faded into lighter and darker blues effortlessly, all of it softening together like weaving a story.

After tonight, I wasn't sure what tale they told.

I tried to decipher it from the tiled roof outside the window of the room we'd taken at the tavern in Lumin. After getting Vale back here and swiping the sweat from her face with a damp cloth, I'd sat beside her bed for a while. She wasn't stirring, though, and the room was stifling. Choking me.

Instead, I'd crawled onto the first story roof our room overlooked. I sat against the wall beside the open window so I'd hear any noise she made and watched the stars.

Why had they given her this fate? What had they written for her that was causing such torment?

She deserved better. Every time she was taken by her sessions' seizing, I'd thought that. She was only trying to help my friends. No matter how angry I was with her, no matter that she would leave, I could acknowledge that she was going out of her way—endangering herself—to assist in the emblem hunt.

"Fucking Angels." I dragged a hand down my face.

As I asked the universe these pressing questions, I tried to wave off the thought that Vale might be doing this for me, too.

Because she knew how much I depended on my friends. Months ago, on the eve of Daminius, I'd torn down my walls and shown her how much I *needed* them all to survive this.

THERE WAS ONLY one place I could go right now. One person who could find some kind of answer to the desperation that had been clawing through my chest since Santorina shared that passage about the Angelcurse a few days prior.

There is no cure but blood for seraphs kissed by Angels. Death is the ultimate sacrifice.

Death. Ophelia's death.

She couldn't fucking die. That wasn't an option.

Malakai had lost any semblance of control when Rina read that aloud. Jezebel had nearly devolved right there on the floor of Lucidius's study, rage and denial bursting from her small frame. Santorina went quiet, and that was almost the worst one. I didn't know how to help silence.

Erista had taken Jezebel, and everyone else who was not as personally tied to Ophelia left, so it was just Malakai, Rina, and me.

They were near opposites in their fear. Mali stormed and huffed around the room. Rina reeled every drop in, answering with a sharp tongue when prodded.

And I'd held on to them. We sat there trying to find answers for hours, until we were too exhausted to continue, then began again the next day. We'd found nothing. But I held on because it already felt like Ophelia was slipping away from us all with this Angelcurse. We couldn't lose someone else.

And Tolek...

Damien's cursed fucking Spirit, I didn't know how Tolek would respond to Ophelia's approaching doom, but it wouldn't be good.

That was why I was knocking on Vale's door now, hours after the sun went down, on the eve of Daminius.

"Cypherion?" she greeted, surprised.

I didn't think the curiosity was about me being here—we'd been sneaking into each other's rooms for weeks, because I didn't want to answer my friends' questions yet.

No, it was likely no surprise that I was here. But a surprise that I was here now.

"I need your help," I confessed.

Vale stepped aside and let me into her suite, leading me straight to the bed chamber and the couches forming a semi-circle before the fire.

"What's wrong?" she asked, immediately adding, "Sorry, that's a stupid question." She tugged her silk robe tighter around her shoulders.

I slumped into a seat, my elbows braced on my knees and my head in my hands.

"Cypherion," she said my name again softly. Always my full name. I loved the way she said it, any way she chose to, but when she said it in that quiet voice, it felt intimate. Like she wasn't only saying it but looking at me. Truly looking.

"I need you to read about the Angelcurse." And then I was pacing before the fire, the words fast and uncontrollable. "I need help—I need an answer, to be able to go back to my friends with a plan because they are all fucking losing it, and I need to hold them together right now." I shoved my hands through my hair, tugging at the ends.

"Ophelia definitely knows about this Angelcurse if she had Santorina searching," I said, "but I also know she doesn't have a plan or she would have come to us. So, I need to find the plan." I stopped, bracing both hands on the mantle and watching the fire.

"I need to give them a way to keep their pieces together or we're all going to disintegrate along with her.

"We lost Malakai once, and it nearly pried Ophelia from us. We only held on to her because the rest of us gave into the denial and accepted his death." I shook my head. "It gave us a false foundation. We tried to carry on, but that damaged all of us in one way or another. None of us are the same people we were when he left. But what happens when another piece of a still-healing foundation is permanently ripped away?"

My voice cracked on that last word.

"We won't survive it, and I fucking need them, Vale. I need them," I admitted, turning to her. "Help me, please."

Vale rose, standing toe to toe with me, over a foot shorter but her stare searing down to my soul. And it was a sad fucking stare.

"I don't know what I can do."

"Please. Try. See if there's a way out of this." Every word I spoke was painfully vulnerable. Some instinct in my head told me not to say anymore. Not to further confess how desperate and lost I was.

Vale's eyes flicked to mine, a war being fought in her gaze. Then, she assessed her table of various reading supplies that I was only beginning to understand the uses of. Her shoulders sank, but she turned back to me.

"I'll do whatever I can."

She led me to a chair, and I sat on nervous pins as she silently attempted readings. For hours we remained in that smoke, and each time she was unable to pull an answer from the Fates.

We spent the entire night together. First with her readings, then in her bed. I worshipped her body, showing her exactly how grateful I was for her help, and when she fell asleep and promised she'd keep trying, there was a bit of a regretful limp to her words.

I hadn't understood then that it was guilt.

And in the morning, when she told me that she'd be returning to Valyn after Daminius as per the agreement between Ophelia and the chancellors—when I thought my chest would cave *in because I was losing someone else now, too—I left without a word.*

~

I'll do whatever I can, she had said. Five words that haunted me months later. Made it impossible to let her in again.

Vale hadn't truly tried. She'd sabotaged those readings—ruined any chance of glimpsing that the Engrossians were about to sack the city, too—and given me hope rather than tell me an ugly truth.

And then, she was just going to leave.

It had been the fist through whatever story the damn stars were writing for us at the time. One I hadn't been able to let go of, months later.

I believed now that she didn't mean to harm the Mystiques with her secrets. I understood it was Titus's manipulation holding her hostage. But when we were done with this mission, Vale was going to leave again, and who would she take out in her wake next time?

I stared at the moon, begging its luminescence to burn the image of her bare beneath me on that night from my mind. Erase every memory of what she'd said, too.

All of that...and she'd been hiding things.

She hadn't had a choice.

And why shouldn't she lie to me? It was easy to be angry with her about it when we were in the mountains or traversing the continent. Seeing her here was different. This territory tore her up, and she wiped scars away every time, like stray tears.

I sighed, tipping my head back against the wall.

Immediately after the Battle of Damenal, I hadn't necessarily believed she had no hand in lying. I thought when we returned here, that secret would be exposed, too. She'd be back to life as it had been, but after tonight, I couldn't keep trying to believe that lie.

Not only was her power turning on her, but the land itself was jumbling her thoughts. Perhaps Vale was as confused as I was.

Weren't we all just a bit lost? Comprised of pieces of broken dreams lodged inside of us like shattered stars careening through the heavens.

"May I join you?" I hadn't even heard her wake up, but just as she had been that night, Vale was there. And I didn't know how to decipher the defensive hunger in my bones at seeing her now.

CHAPTER ELEVEN
CYPHERION

Vale's voice was a bell through the night as she poked her head out the window. It called to something in my chest as it always had.

"Of course," I said, scrambling to rise and give her my hand as she sat on the ledge and swung her legs over, bare from toe to thigh despite the chill. She'd changed out of her sweat-stained outfit from the rings, wearing a similar blue chiffon one now.

She must have visited the bathing chamber and splashed water on her face, too, if the curling, damp strands of hair framing her wide eyes were any sign.

"How are you feeling?" I asked, watching her closely for hints of the lies I'd learned to pick apart.

Vale bent her head, studying her rings. A wave of hair slipped across her face, and without thinking, I tucked it behind her ear.

Fuck. I shouldn't be doing that.

I *couldn't* be taking those small steps, little actions that would make things easier between us. Closer. I couldn't let her in again. Nothing that had happened tonight changed that.

Fear had been a cold snake woven between my ribs, and I didn't have room for it. I cared about enough people in mortal danger. Five. Tolek, Malakai, Ophelia, Santorina, and Jezebel. That was all I needed or wanted.

Still, when I'd seen her so weak and vulnerable, that Starsearcher's hands on her, I'd been lost.

And when I touched her now, my skin tingled. Vale's sharp inhale said she felt it, too. So responsive. She'd always been that way.

"I'm all right. Tired, but better than usual after..."

Sometimes it took her days to recover from an episode, but she really did appear okay now. Skin and eyes brighter, limbs not shaky.

Turning to face her, I said, "We—"

"Your head," Vale gasped.

My brows pulled together, and—"Fuck, ouch." I winced as the slice to my eyebrow throbbed. "I forgot about it."

Vale fought a smirk. "Forgot you had a head wound?"

"There were important things happening." The blood staining my cheek was probably gory in the moonlight. The cut was likely almost healed over by now, just tender. It had been a deep one, though. More of a mess than anything. "I'll go wash up."

"No," Vale said, pushing to her feet with a firm hand on my shoulder. "Let me."

She disappeared inside and was back before I could say anything, towels both damp and dry in hand. She carried a myriad of other supplies that I hadn't realized she had with her.

I wanted to ask where she got them. Wanted to know more about what happened tonight. But Vale crouched down in front of me, practically sitting in my lap to reach the cut. When her ass rested gently on my thigh, I couldn't form a damn sentence.

And then she raised the damp towel to dab at my forehead. Gentle fingers picked away the reminders of the night, close enough that each of her breaths fanned across my cheek, loud in the silence. I closed my eyes and inhaled, trying to focus on anything other than where she was so warm in my lap and dig up a semblance of sense.

"Thank you," Vale said, swapping a wet cloth for a dry one.

I swallowed over my dry throat. "For?"

Where was I supposed to put my hands? I couldn't grip her hips, but they hung useless at my sides now, tapping the tile.

"For coming for me tonight." She dragged the cloth down my cheek where the blood had dripped, her touch so careful yet confident, as she was in everything we did. "I felt safer when you arrived."

My eyes flicked open, brows rising, and I hissed at the pain of that action. Vale gave me a scolding look. I almost laughed, but something about her gratitude bothered me.

"You shouldn't thank someone for caring for you, Vale."

Because I did care.

I shouldn't.

I didn't want to.

But I did, only a little bit. She was easy to care for, and there was no person on Ambrisk that deserved Vale's thanks for something as simple as that.

Her chest rose at my words, putting her breasts right in my face beneath that thin chiffon, and I closed my eyes to focus on anything besides her. She felt...nervous. Could someone *feel* nervous? That was how her thigh barely daring to touch mine felt as her fingers continued to clean the slice to my head.

"It needs to be sewn up," she finally said. "With something that deep, it might reopen before magic can heal it."

"I'll find someone tomo—"

"I can do it." Vale sat back a bit, giving us both room to breathe. "If that's okay. I have supplies here. I bought them at the market."

"You know how to do that?" I asked.

"I've stitched many things in my life." She didn't elaborate, but I knew it was about the temple. She always had a slightly different tone to her voice when she spoke of it.

I was there for four years.
We were punished if our readings were not clear enough.
My friends and I snuck to each others' rooms at night.
The brand on my shoulder...

Each was said with a certain inflection, despite the gravity of the confession. Each was a piece of herself offered after being burned so many times. Pieces, I was realizing, I could never fully turn away, no matter how hard I tried.

"Go ahead," I said. "But talk to me as you do it. Please."

And now it was the inflection in my words that she was reading. The way I said *please*, desperately and vulnerably, as I had that night I came to her begging for help.

Clearly, as we locked eyes in silence, both of us were taken back there. Both of us acknowledged what happened, accepting it without needing to say it.

"What do you want me to talk about?" Vale asked, digging through her supplies.

I needed something heavy. Not frivolous. That wouldn't be enough of a distraction.

"Who is Harlen?" I asked.

Vale froze for the briefest moment, then stood, a sterilized needle and Bodymelder thread in hand. She crept closer and assessed the way I was seated against the wall. Looked at the tiled roof around us and judged the angle of the light.

"May I?" she asked, gesturing to my lap.

My throat dried again. I nodded, and she positioned herself across my hips, firmly straddling me. Great.

As she dug the needle in for the first stitch, she started speaking, and her voice became that wind chime that carried away the pain. "Harlen and I were at the Lumin Temple together. I've told you a bit about...my time there."

I was sure she left out the most horrific parts, but there'd been violence against the children at the hands of the masters. Her brand was from the temple.

"Was he—" I hissed as she tugged at the thread. Reflexively, my hands shot to her hips.

She froze for a moment, then relaxed against me, bringing her that much closer. I held on.

"Don't talk, or you'll move, and it'll hurt more," she scolded. I liked that firm tone while she sat like this more than I should.

"Harlen was not branded as I was. He was an orphan who turned to the temple for help, but we arrived the same week. As I've said, I've told you a bit about my time at the temple, though I haven't elaborated on *why* I was there in the first place or why I left."

Tug, tug, tug, that needle went against my skin, and she unfolded her story between us. She spoke calmly, but this was something she was trusting me with. Something she offered after what I did for her tonight.

"Back then, the masters were taking children in secret. It was illegal, but some didn't care. Villages were ransacked, children were branded to temples, some faced much worse fates." The end of her sentence faltered, and I could only imagine why. "At first, I didn't know why I was taken. It wasn't until I was older that I learned I was sent to the temple because I was deemed special. Starsearchers' readings are not only tied to our Angel, but—"

"They depend on the eleven Fates," I said, hissing again as the thread pulled.

"Shh," she reprimanded with a slight laugh. "But yes. The eleven Fates—used to be twelve—are our touchpoints leading to Valyrie and Moirenna." She paused. "You really remember?"

I remember everything, I'd told her before the night went to the Spirits in the fighting rings.

Vale stopped stitching this time and let me move my lips very carefully, leaning closer to her. My hands tightened on her hips with the motion.

"All of it. And I've done my own research."

More than I would admit.

"Well, then you remember how Starsearchers each align with a certain Fate as we grow into mature warriors."

"Yes," I mumbled, gently massaging my thumbs into her hips. Having her settled across my lap was an acute form of torture. There was no way she couldn't feel how hard I was through my leathers. "Usually, the alignment with a Fate has to do with the time of year a Starsearcher is born or the positioning of the stars, but there are apparently cases when—"

"I'm aligned to nine."

"Nine?" I nearly shouted, my eyes shooting open. Luckily, Vale had been prepared for that reaction and had tied and cut the stitches before she said it.

She moved to climb off my lap, but I held her hips tighter. "Isn't being aligned with even two fates rare, Vale?"

She nodded slowly. My mind whirled, trying to track down pieces that made this make any sense.

Cruelty and Adoration, she'd once told me. But for my spirit, I couldn't remember a time she said that was her only tie. Only that she received powerful readings from the Fate. So carefully deceptive with her words.

"So, what does that mean?" I asked, ignoring the discomfort from that reminder.

"It means..." She took a deep breath, let it out slowly and sank into me. "It means that when City Council learned of a powerful young searcher in their town—before even all nine Fate ties had revealed themselves—they reported it to Lumin Temple. And the masters collected me from my family when I was four. I suffered at their hands for four years before Titus caught wind of my existence and rescued me...or took me?"

Her words tilted up at the end, like she still wasn't sure how to finish that sentence. I knew how I wanted to. My fingers dug into her hips at the thought of the chancellor beneath my scythe.

Of any of them. This council or the temple masters. The

latter were within reach. I could go now, make them regret ever laying a fucking hand on her. I had enough blades in the room for each of them to receive their own, surely.

Vale's palm cupped my cheek, pulling me from the murderous intention I shouldn't be having over her.

"I think my connection to nine is tied to why we're here, though."

And that reminder was a cool splash of water over me.

"Right," I said, swallowing the anger. "Nine fates, messed up readings. There must be a connection. Who knows of your alignment?"

For a moment, hurt flashed through her eyes at my abruptness, and she stiffened.

I didn't move her off me, though. She seemed to be waiting for it, but after tonight—after the truths she'd just given me—I took a break in pushing her away. I wanted her as close as possible.

So, I dragged my hands up her sides, around her ribs, and back down, repeating the action until she met my gaze. "Give me all the pieces, Stargirl, so we can figure this out together."

That name relaxed her, something uncoiling within me in turn. A bit of my leash slipping.

"Harlen didn't know." Spirits bless her for knowing he'd still be in the back of my mind. "None of the children at the temple with me knew, and as far as I understand, when Titus brought me on as his apprentice, only he knew."

"He made you his apprentice at eight years old?"

She nodded. "I started reading for him immediately. The official declaration came only a few months later, and he inked over the brand shortly after that."

At the reminder, my hand slid to that tattoo. Hatred curdled in my chest because of what it did to her. How she felt a twisted loyalty to it, how she still felt obligated to please Titus because he'd overridden her debt to the temple masters.

"And I was beholden to him." Vale took a huge breath

before continuing, seeming almost painfully conflicted. "That's why I couldn't go against his wishes to sabotage my readings or confess that I'm aligned to nine Fates. He saved me from so many horrors, and he knows about my Fate ties. I don't know what they mean, but I can't turn away that relationship."

How much of a relationship did they truly have? While Titus had freed her, was a different captor really a worthy solution?

One thing was clear: I needed to uncover what the chancellor was up to. Something about Vale's entire story didn't settle right within me.

But that wasn't important right now.

She continued, "I thought about defying him sometimes, but every time I was about to, I heard his voice reminding me how dangerous my secret was."

Brushing across the tattooed brand, I wound a strand of her hair around my finger. Spun it and let go, continuing my journey down her arm until I found her hand. Then, I interlocked our fingers.

"Why are you telling me now?" I asked.

"Because tonight I realized that maybe Titus isn't the one with my best intentions at heart." She blinked back tears, her grip curling around mine. "Titus hasn't written to me since Daminius, Cypherion. The letters have all been from someone else. I don't recognize the handwriting, but it isn't his."

There was such a vulnerable abandonment in her voice—it was the most she'd ever let her walls down.

Fury burned through me. "He deserted you?"

After using her, he left her to our discretion—a clan she had deceived. That fucking *protector* left her.

"I don't know." Admitting that seemed to weigh her down, so I bit back every accusation I wanted to let soar and instead tilted her chin up to look at me.

"We're going to figure it out, Vale," I promised. "What it means, why your sessions are hurting you, and how it ties back to Ophelia. I swear, we're going to get the answers you deserve. You've lived far too long without them."

Warning flared in the back of my mind at the sincerity in my words, the brightening of her eyes, and the way I *liked* seeing her happy. But for the moment, I told it to shut up. Now that Vale and I had been forced to talk about parts of this mess, it was harder to hate her. Harder to pretend I didn't care.

With the way her confession about Titus's abandonment ignited fury within me, I knew that was a losing battle.

The fucking chancellor…

He'd been manipulating her all these years.

"I'm sorry I never told you," Vale said, and I froze.

"What?" I asked.

"I'm sorry," she repeated. She seemed to deflate at saying those words. "About the Fates and my past and Titus's rules. I wanted to, but I thought Titus would somehow know. Being back here, though…I've realized that I'm so small. And my movements don't upset the balance as I thought they did. And if I'd realized that sooner, I would have told you everything."

"Some of that is right," I said. "You're not some small thing in the universe, though. You should be free to make decisions without being beholden to him, but you have a connection to *nine Fates* when most Starsearchers only have one. That's not small, Vale. You aren't unimportant to the universe."

She was reinstating herself as the center of mine, and that was a problem for another night, when we weren't both bloodied and broken. Tonight, I wanted to set down the armor. I wanted to rest knowing she was safe and admit to myself that fact mattered.

"I'm still sorry…"

"That's the first time you've said that," I said.

She blinked those wide olive eyes. "What?"

"In all of these months since the Battle of Damenal, you haven't once told me you were sorry."

"Did you think I wasn't?"

"Yes," I admitted. "For a while, I thought you'd only ever meant to use me and leave. That you didn't care what your lies risked. And until now, I didn't know what to think. Because you never said a word."

"I mean it," she said, and she shifted closer to me, our chests brushing together. Her hands came around the back of my neck. "I *am* sorry, and I'm sorry I didn't say it sooner. I'm sorry for both of us that I didn't start asking questions sooner. And I'm sorry for my role in allowing Damenal to be sacked. For not trying to see it ahead of time and fortifying the borders as we could have. I'm sorry for putting the people you love at risk, because I know how much your life is wound to theirs, and I'm sorry for getting us here."

Her lips were only a breath from mine. She was so close that I couldn't pick apart every apology she'd just made. I was certain there were some in there that I needed to comment on, but Spirits, it was hard to think with her against me. I could see the individual streaks of color in her eyes. Could smell nothing but starlight.

Was it possible for someone to smell like starlight? That's what I always thought of when Vale was close to me. Like a clear midnight sky, free and promising, and that scent consumed me now. It was all over her, I remembered. Couldn't forget. She even tasted like it.

That wasn't something I should be thinking about now. Not as she was leaning closer and our lips would brush if I tilted my head at just the right angle.

Instead, I stood, locking her legs around my hips. "Let's go to bed. It's been a long night."

I carried her through the window because I didn't believe she wasn't still exhausted. Not because I wanted to hold her longer. Definitely not.

This was best for both of us. Our emotions weren't steady after everything tonight. We needed to recover. To think. To reassess.

When I finally set her on the floor, she laughed.

"What?" I asked, latching the window behind us.

Vale inclined her head, the smile on her lips slicing through my chest.

Looking over her shoulder, I grumbled, "There's always only one fucking bed."

~

I MADE Vale take the bed again and settled on my sleeping mat.

The fire crackled beside my head as I laid on my back, eyes locked on the ceiling and mind replaying everything she'd said.

"Cypherion Kastroff." Vale's voice cut through the room, impatient and admonishing. I propped myself on an elbow to meet her eyes, glowing in the dark. "Stop being such a stubborn ass, and sleep in the damn bed."

CHAPTER TWELVE
VALE

FATES BE DAMNED, HE LAUGHED.

It was so quiet, I thought I'd imagined it at first, but Cypherion shook his head as he chuckled.

"That's not a good idea," he said, voice rough, and he flopped down on his back again.

"Why not?" I asked, scurrying to the end of the bed where I could still see him.

"Because." He watched the ceiling adamantly.

"Because..."

Cypherion considered for a moment, searching the low wooden beams. The air thickened with each second he didn't speak, heavy indecision and something akin to longing clouding between us. Finally, he sighed, "Because, Vale, I only have so much restraint."

His words went right through me, burning straight to my core. Flashes of memories—of teeth and lips and tongues against skin, of cries of pleasure and him filling me—ignited a familiar ache within me.

But there was something in his tone that hurt enough to dull that longing. A sense of sadness that said he did not *want* to want those things with me.

"I'm not going to tempt you into anything, Cypherion," I promised, but I couldn't keep the scorn from seeping into my voice.

He heard it. I knew he did based on the way his eyes flicked back to mine and regret bathed the blues.

We stayed like that for a moment, watching one another, and the heartbreak gathered between us.

Him begging me for answers.

Me failing to provide them.

Him staying with me that night.

Me telling him I was leaving as dawn broke.

"Okay, Stargirl," he finally said.

And then, he was moving around the other side of the bed, and I was scrambling back beneath the covers.

We both lay there silently for a moment, watching the ceiling. Memories from Damenal collected between us, him coming for me in the fighting ring tonight piling above that, and words and secrets exchanged on the roof topping it all.

I'd told him of my Fate ties. Of how unlikely and coveted they were, of how I didn't know what it meant. Perhaps I shouldn't have, but a piece of my riling heart had settled as I did. And maybe a piece of him did, too. A sliver that wanted answers, that wanted to understand why I'd kept secrets.

"What's it like?" he asked finally, deep voice soothing in the darkness. "Nine Fates."

"It's...heavy," I explained. "I'm used to it, because it's all I've known. But the first time I realized it was abnormal was when everyone else would talk about the silent stretches. Sometimes, they go days without feeling the need to read. My Fates are louder, always calling me. And when I have a tenuous grip on the power as I have recently, it's harder to keep a wall between reality and their realm."

"Their realm?" Cypherion rolled onto his side to face me.

I canted my head toward him, my hair fanning out across

the pillow. "Just as there's a Spirit Realm and other worlds in existence, it is assumed the celestial powers have one."

He considered. "But you like your magic, despite how heavy it is?"

"I love it," I assured him, turning onto my side eagerly. "It's difficult at times, but it's mine. It's strength and purpose and direction." Even if I was misguided now, my magic was the polestar I returned to, the thing that ran life through my veins.

"I've always wondered what that's like," Cypherion said.

"What *what's* like?"

"To be so certain about your role."

"Is this about your title?" I asked. When he declined to answer, I continued, "Cypherion, did you notice how not one person in that war room had anything to say against Ophelia's appointment of you? Not one person thought she was making a mistake. Don't convince yourself she is."

"Stargirl..." He sighed. Tentatively, he reached up to tuck a piece of hair behind my ear. It was so gentle—a touch he hadn't expressed for months, but one I craved. "It's so much more than that."

"I know you're scared because of your father. I know you're worried because you feel like a part of you is missing." He'd told me enough about his family before Daminius for me to put the pieces together. At my words, his hand paused, cupping my cheek, and I whispered pleadingly, "But see the good in yourself that the rest of us do."

"I think I'm still finding it," he admitted, voice low. His hand drifted lower, thumb stroking over my pulse point.

"Let me help you." I shifted closer to him. He'd been intoxicating as I stitched his wound. His large hands on my hips with a searing ownership, thumbs stroking over my ribs, like it was the only thing rooting him to the moment. His hard length pressed against my center with a shift of my hips.

Perhaps it had been a horrid idea.

It took every ounce of strength not to lean into him then

because I remembered. I remembered his lips tracing every inch of my skin. As I thought of it now, my body heated.

I squirmed beneath the blankets, and Cypherion stilled, eyes dropping as if understanding what was going through my mind. When he lifted his gaze, the blues deepened with a want so potent, it swallowed the air around us.

"Vale," he sighed.

Please, I wanted to beg. *Please don't put up a wall. Don't leave me as so many have. Please just be here now, with me, in whatever capacity you can.*

It was on the tip of his tongue, I thought. To say *"fuck the rules"* and devour me. It was in his searing stare, in the gentle drop of his hand down my ribs, his thumb coasting over my nipple as it pebbled against the silk.

But I wouldn't say any of it. I would not break my promise of tempting him.

"Fuck," he breathed, his gaze following the repeated movement. I nearly whimpered with restraint at the sound of his voice, so husky and desiring.

"Fuck, Vale." He exhaled again, and I held my breath. His fingers toyed with the fabric of my nightgown, slipping under the strap, but not pulling it down. "Say something," he begged.

"I said I wasn't going to tempt you." My voice was shaky. "The decision is yours."

"Your entire existence is a temptation, Stargirl." My breath caught in my throat as he gently pulled the strap down my arm a few inches and hovered over me. "Every time you speak, every room you walk into, I fight myself. Seeing you and knowing I can't have you again destroys me."

"I'm here, though."

"You are now." His hand coasted over my breast and down my stomach, toying with the hem of my nightgown. "You won't always be."

Those words, and the broken resolve in them, stuck to the back of my throat.

I didn't know what the end of this journey would bring for me. For us. What the Fates would reveal if—or when—we fixed my readings.

Spirits, I didn't even know what tomorrow would bring, what promises I could make to him.

His fingers danced up the inside of my thigh, and I wanted so badly for him to move them to my center. To feel him inside of me again so we could forget all the pain the world drove between us and just be in this moment.

Maybe if neither of us had ever been hurt, we could have.

Cypherion watched as his fingers drifted closer to my core. My breathing quickened with anticipation. Just as he reached the apex of my thighs, his stare met mine, searching.

I didn't know what he saw, but whatever it was had his eyes falling closed. His hand retreated, and his lips dropped to my forehead.

"Go to sleep, Stargirl," he muttered.

And though my heart clenched in my chest at all the possibilities slipping through our fingers, I tried my best to sleep.

At some point, his arm found its way back to my waist, pulling me tightly against him, and we woke still like that in the morning.

Chapter Thirteen
Cypherion

It had been a mistake. Vale and I in the same bed. Waking up with her ass pressed against my cock, the slightest shift driving me wild.

That thing that had relied on her and trusted her woke up with the dawn this morning, and I'd spent the entire walk to the blood orange grove on the southern border of Lumin trying to banish it again.

Though, I was beginning to doubt it ever truly left.

"We can't wait much longer," I said, crossing my arms and leaning back against a tree.

Vale stretched up for an orange, dancing on her toes to reach the lowest branches, and swore in a hard voice, "He'll come."

"He might not," I said. "And perhaps that's for the best. We need to figure out what that reading meant and get moving." I'd allowed us both to get distracted last night, but I couldn't do that anymore.

Vale stiffened. "We—"

"Careful," a voice I'd much rather *not* hear echoed around the trees. That Starsearcher—Harlen—rounded the trunk, tucking his hands into his pockets. "She has a rather nasty bite, from what I recall."

"Hi, Harls," Vale said softly. A selfish part of me hated the hope in her eyes when she said his name. I stifled a groan.

Why was she trusting him to know we were here?

He strode over to her, plucking a blood orange from the tree and tossing it up with a cocky smirk. "Hi, Vale."

"You got my note?"

"It found me." He grimaced, holding up the slip of parchment crumpled in his hand. A smug satisfaction warmed my chest.

"Not a fan of Mystique ink?" I asked.

"It's...invasive. That sort of magic is unnatural to me," Harlen retorted, tucking away the parchment. "But I suppose it did me a favor today." His eyes found Vale's again, and when he beamed, I couldn't stifle my scoff.

Vale cut me a harsh glare. "We made a deal," she reminded me.

I grumbled beneath my breath, regretting my agreement to make this detour to discuss whatever it was she wanted with Harlen before we carried on with Ophelia's mission.

This Starsearcher hadn't seen Vale in sixteen years, and though they'd been friends as children, he looked at her like she was a prize. And Vale *was* a prize, in a way. But she was something to be cherished, not something to be won.

Stop thinking like that, Kastroff.

Harlen wrapped an arm around Vale's shoulders, tucking her to him, and all I could think about was my hands on her hips last night. Her in that nightgown and how easy it would have been to slide the straps down. The feel of her breasts through the fabric and the heat between her thighs.

I'd been so close to shoving aside the last scraps of lace and silk and diving into her.

She's leaving.

Shaking away the thought, I trained my vision on Harlen as he took out a triple blade and sliced an orange.

"I should have known this was where you'd want to meet," he said, handing Vale a piece. "The grove thrives in winter."

When she bit into it, she hummed, and it went straight through me.

"*Fuck*," I breathed, so quietly I didn't think they heard. I'd never withstand this mission if she kept sounding like that.

Vale straightened, wiping her hands on her skirt and taking a step back from Harlen. Guard up. So perhaps she was a bit more wary about this meeting than she let on.

Vale settled on the grass, not seeming to mind the winter-chilled earth. Silently, I slid down the trunk and propped my arms on my bent knees.

"I wanted to thank you for helping me last night," Vale began, and Harlen nodded. "How long have you been back here?"

With a sigh, the Starsearcher sat, still swinging his knife between two fingers. He moved gracefully, at one with the sway of the branches. "I never left."

"You haven't?" Her eyes widened, and I took in every small movement—every subtle tilt of her head and intake of breath—to gauge how difficult this topic was for her.

"Not for longer than a few weeks. Short trips here and there."

"Why?"

"Lumin is my home." He said it simply, as if she'd agree, but Vale's face remained impassive. "When I turned of age and finished my studies and tests, I found work. I rent an apartment near the market. I travel when I need to. It's a good life."

"But the things we experienced..."

"Nothing was worse than the day you left, Vale. After that, I didn't care about any of it."

A sharp intake of breath. Behind her olive eyes, her guard slipped. "What?"

"I was a little boy who had only ever known one friend in the world, and one morning, she disappeared. No explanation, no goodbye. After that, all I had was this city and myself. I had to make my own home."

"You could have gone anywhere," Vale said.

"I go places." Harlen shrugged, watching the silver blade swing in his hand. "I feel a sort of loyalty to my younger self. I haven't wanted to leave."

A bit of my frustration with the Starsearcher chipped away at his confession. Only the smallest chunk, but enough that I was able to understand what he meant. I'd been just as lost as him before. And I could respect that loyalty—reluctantly.

"But there's so much more out there," Vale said, voice layered with sadness for the boy Harlen had once been. "You can get away from—"

"I don't want to get away from it," he roared, and I shifted closer to Vale but didn't comment. Sighing, Harlen continued, "I'm sorry. I didn't mean that. But...what are *you* doing here?"

His eyes flicked between the two of us, questioning.

"I—" Vale began and then froze.

He didn't know about her sessions, and from the way she snapped her mouth closed, I guessed she didn't want to tell him. So, I blurted, "Revered Alabath sent us on a mission for the good of the Mystique Warriors and the alliance clans."

Vale's head snapped toward me.

Harlen perked up. "The war is over. The battles ceased—"

"The battles ceased in the southern mountains because the Engrossian queen was killed," I said, tone not brokering argument. "But the war is far from over. What Vale and I search for is not to be disclosed."

"*Second* Kastroff is right," Vale added, emphasizing my title in a way that made my jaw tick. "I cannot tell you more. But that is why I'm here, and I'll be leaving as soon as possible."

Leaving?

A bead of hope tried to bloom in my chest.

"And when this mysterious task is over, where will you go?" Harlen challenged. For the sake of my Spirit, why did he care? Couldn't he let her go?

"I'll go...home." Vale sighed as she said it, and that bead of hope in my chest extinguished with the breath.

To Valyn. She'd leave when we were done, but she'd return to Valyn.

Harlen pushed to his feet, and we both followed. He rushed toward Vale, and my hand twitched to my knife.

A million questions burned in the Starsearcher's stare. A million things he wanted to say.

But he didn't.

Spirits, did I know how that felt. I dropped my hand, but held my stance.

Harlen's eyes flicked between us accusingly, but instead of arguing, he stepped back. "Well, I guess this is goodbye, then. I see you're in good hands, and I won't keep you."

With that, he was through the trees and gone.

And Vale didn't follow him. She stood there with her hands fisted at her sides and her chin lifted in the determination she wore so fiercely. But her expressive face told me the truth. The tremble of her lips, the quick blinks.

"Vale, I—"

Whirling, she stepped right up to me. "Thank you for the intervention, but in the future, I can handle those matters myself."

"Pardon?" My brows shot up, tugging at the fresh stitches.

"I wouldn't have told Harlen anything confidential." She crossed her arms, tilting her chin up. Her waves tumbled around her shoulders, and a breeze wrapped her scent through the grove. I tried to focus on what she was saying rather than the alluring way her slender throat worked as she swallowed and glared at me. "He may have been my closest friend many years ago, but I knew better than to reveal Ophelia's secrets to someone we don't know."

"I didn't think you were going to," I said quickly. "I only thought it might be less questionable coming from someone he didn't know."

And she'd seemed uncomfortable under his interrogation. But I didn't think she'd pour out our secrets so easily.

"Vale, I..." I sighed, shoving my hands into my pockets. "I've come to trust you with the information we've gathered." Not as I once had, but since the Seawatcher trial on those platforms in the ocean—since she'd helped me during the alpheous attack, all the way until last night when she'd confided in me—Vale had been steadily winning back my trust, despite my wishes.

She blinked those large eyes at me, chin pulling back, a bit affronted, I thought, but I wasn't sure why.

"Fine," she finally said, storming through the trees.

Her skirt swished as she disappeared among the fronds, and it took me a moment to catch up.

"What about the second half of our deal?" I asked, taking long strides to reach her. I tried to keep my voice as light as possible. "You can't avoid it. We need to figure out what the searcher meant last night. About the ninth level."

"We don't need to figure anything out," Vale growled, swiping vines out of her way as the jungle grew denser. I thought she was walking aimlessly, just getting out whatever tension the interaction with Harlen had sprouted, but I followed regardless.

"Yes, we do." I gripped her shoulder, tugging her to a stop and spinning her to face me. "I know this is all a sensitive topic and your magic is betraying you. I know you hate being here, Vale, and trust me, I understand." She watched her feet, toying with a large frond that draped across the path. The dullness in her eyes sliced through my heart like a hot blade.

Curse myself and that side of me that didn't want her to hurt. Tilting her chin up to me, I waited for her to meet my eyes.

"Maybe I don't understand it because I can't feel it the way you do, but I can see it. And I know that I'm enraged every time I see that damn temple and think about what happened to you within it. And I'm scared about the way your magic is threatening you. But we have to fight past those fears, because we need answers."

She froze, blinking up at me. And I was taken back to nights in Damenal when she looked at me like I was the first truth she'd ever learned in her life. Like I was more than just a warrior, but someone to trust. Someone to believe in.

"I wasn't going to give Harlen confidential information," she repeated. "I appreciate your defense. I think I just wanted to see him again to see if...any of home remained."

It was a peace offering. A thought in exchange for the reassurance I'd offered.

"I understand," I agreed. Vale longed for home and the innocence that had been ripped from her too soon. Harlen was a vital piece of that.

"And we don't need answers because I know what the Starsearcher meant," Vale whispered, lips barely moving. I bent lower to hear what she said next, my heart pounding. "The ninth floor below the archives. That's what she said. That's where we'll find what we need."

"Which archives, though?" My hand tightened briefly on her shoulder, but I dropped it and stepped back. I was supposed to be keeping my distance, and that speech I'd just given was certainly not doing that. I dragged a hand through my hair and tried to breathe normally. "Are they in the..."

I didn't want to say temple.

"The ninth floor is a clue for me. Because of the Fates I'm drawn to." She swallowed. "And the archives she's referencing are the Valyn Citadel Archives."

My heart crashed through my chest.

Valyn.

The Starsearcher capital.

Where Titus was.

"We have to go to Valyn?" I mumbled, hands fisting at my sides.

"We have to go to Valyn," she confirmed, voice as numb as the words made me feel.

~

Vale had gone dull during the journey from Lumin to Valyn, like her starlight winked out.

I hoped getting her away from the temple would restore a bit of her confidence, like what she'd found during the hunt for the emblems as she stood up for herself.

Something was stopping her, though.

And despite everything I swore, every boundary I promised myself I'd restore, it was driving me crazy.

"Did you have friends in Valyn that you'd like to see when we're there?" It was a pointless offer. We couldn't make our presence obvious if we didn't want Titus to know we were in the capital. And with how elusive his moves had been—how he hadn't written to her once—it was best if we concealed ourselves.

But if she needed it, I could find a way.

"I did not have friends," she deadpanned. Her voice didn't sound like a bell anymore. "I rarely left the chancellor's manor due to my work."

"None?" I should have stopped pushing her, but she was speaking at least. That was better than an evasive silence.

Vale cast a distant stare over her shoulder. "We are not all as fortunate as you, Cypherion."

And I was an ass.

Vale was alone in so many more ways than I'd known, ways she'd implied but had never fully explained because Titus forced her to hide so much. But she'd always watched my friends with a glint of longing in her eye. Now I knew why.

We were all searching for things in our lives. Maybe Vale's was a home. A place to belong. She needed people who truly cared for her.

And she *had* apologized on that roof. For the first time, she'd torn down that wall and sorrow had burned beneath those words.

Perhaps I could be that friend for her, until she left.

It was clear there was too much damage between us to go beyond that, no matter how badly I wanted her. At the end of this, she'd go back to Titus.

I'll go home, she'd said to Harlen. That was her home, wasn't it?

But the prospect of heading back to the capital now had leached color from her face. So why would she return when this was done?

I didn't understand, but I knew when this was over, I'd be in Damenal as Ophelia's Second, Angels willing we all make it there. Until then...

I cleared my throat. "I...I'm your friend, Vale."

"Are you?" It could have been teasing once, months ago. A jokingly arched brow waiting for me to admit I wanted her as more than a friend. But now there was genuine pain lacing her voice.

"Yes," I promised. It took all my power not to nudge Erini forward to Vale's side. "I'm your friend. My friends are your friends now, too."

You're not alone anymore, Stargirl. Don't go back there.

"Thank you," she said, chin down and eyes on her hands. No acknowledgement of that silent pleading.

Vale and I had an end, and the sooner we reached it the better. Until then, we'd be friends, and I'd set aside my other feelings.

~

When we stopped mid-afternoon, I took my time caring for Erini. She was a quiet horse, but a strong one, and the time spent with her was meditative.

Vale was calmly brushing Marage. She unscrewed the top of her canteen and shook it, but nothing came out.

"Here." I offered her mine and some fruit, then stopped to unroll the map I'd been tracking our path on. We could have headed into the jungle and followed the century-worn trails. Erini would have likely found our way to the capital, but plans were important. Going without them when unnecessary was setting yourself up for foolish, avoidable danger.

"Looks like there's a small town just over the next ridge," I said, rolling the map back up. "We can stay there for the night and reach Valyn by sunset tomorrow. If that's okay with you."

"Sure." Vale nodded, eyes and voice hollow. Spirits, I may only be able to be her friend, but I missed her smiles.

"Have you been through this area before?" I asked.

"Not since—" She snapped her mouth shut, regret darkening her cheeks.

Since...

"Vale, are we taking the *same* route?" Her silence was enough of an answer. "Cursed Angels." I pinched between my brows. *Be nice. Be friendly.* "We could have gone the other way around the lake."

We did not have to take the same route she'd traveled with Titus as he took her from the Lumin Temple to Valyn.

"No, we couldn't," she rushed out. "This is the fastest route. It's okay."

"Vale," I pleaded, "don't do this. Don't pretend none of this is bothering you when I only know the slightest of demons you're fighting, and they sure as Spirits are bothering me."

She was shocked into silence for a moment, chewing her lip. "It is rather beautiful out here," she finally said, and the serpent around my heart uncoiled a bit at the energy in her voice.

"Stunning," I said, staring at her, begging her to continue.

"Actually," she contemplated. Her eyes grew so wide and hopeful, but a tinge afraid, like she didn't know what to expect. "I'd like to take you somewhere. If that's okay with you."

If that's okay with you. We were being so delicate with each other, and a piece of me hated it.

"Yeah, Stargirl," I breathed, and with it, I released another bout of the hostility I'd been clinging to. "Anywhere."

Chapter Fourteen
Vale

As we'd crept back toward my cage over the past few days, the stars bore down on me, but I was waking up. I had one last night of freedom. One last chance to grasp the bars and throw them wide before I had to play the game in the capital.

And we'd spend it in the hot springs.

Cypherion's eyes burned into my back as I led him through the narrow, winding jungle trail, but I relished the sting his attention left along my skin.

We'd left the horses at the inn after securing a room in the town near the springs—two beds this time. I was sure he'd be thrilled.

"Are we almost there?" he asked.

"Patience," I answered, but the bubbling water was growing louder, my heartbeat pounding with it. Unable to help myself, I shot him a small smile over my shoulder.

"What is that?" Cypherion asked, his breath fogging in front of him.

I didn't answer, instead picking up my pace and taking the rest of the trail in a few steps.

Sweeping away the last of the plants, I ducked into the secluded, misty clearing and spun toward him. Cypherion's eyes widened, bouncing from the steaming hot spring pools up the cliff to the top of the waterfall.

Trees formed a dense ring around the springs, but the canopy overhead was open, a clear shot to the stars. The rock wall before us formed tiers, a large pool at the base collecting the water from the falls, but smaller pockets of steaming baths nestled in each step.

For some reason, the water was hot here all year round. I'd found this spot as a girl, and any of the few times I was allowed away from Valyn, I took the chance to escape alone here.

Cypherion's eyes widened as he took it in. Nerves fluttered throughout my body, and I sucked in a breath, waiting for him to say something about this secret I'd kept for years.

"This is magnificent, Vale," he finally said, awe-struck, and satisfaction settled my racing heart.

"The water is always warm, so we can swim even in the winter."

His eyes snapped to me then, the blues so deep, an ocean swirling with questions. "I don't…"

I scoffed, turning to the edge of the rock and kicking off my boots. "Don't be so shy, Cypherion."

Keeping my back to him, I untied my cloak, dropping it to the ground. My top, skirt, and undergarments followed, leaving me in nothing but my silver jewelry.

One chance. I had one chance at freedom, one night to indulge. If Cypherion Kastroff was too modest to join me, that was his choice. But the babbling of the falls called to pieces of me I'd long ago kissed goodbye, and I couldn't stifle them tonight.

Looking over my shoulder, I caught him staring at my body, eyes falling over the curve of my waist and ass like hot honey across my skin. It was nothing he hadn't seen before—exalted even—and while he claimed we were *friends,* there was nothing friendly in that stare.

Every inch of me heated in response, desire waking. For his hands on my body, to bite down on his bottom lip. For the pleasure he wrung out of me.

No, I told myself. *He doesn't want that. He doesn't want you.*

And though it broke my heart to remind myself I had let him go, I refused to allow that pain between us to dampen this place.

"Scared, Cypherion?" I teased.

I waded into the water before he could answer, but I thought I heard him mumble something along the lines of "*fucking terrified,*" and I smirked.

The waterfall was slower than most, the babble a hum of music rather than an overbearing drone. It was serene. I ducked beneath the water, surfacing quickly and brushing my hair back from my face.

The heat stung my skin in the most delicious way, soothing not only the sore muscles from days of travel but my worries as well. Taking thoughts of tainted sessions, Angel emblems, and Titus. Here, in this bubble, none of it mattered as I crouched down so the water came to my shoulders and steam swirled about my ears.

The spring's current shifted around me, and I spun.

Cypherion was there, his long hair damp and darker than usual, blue eyes shining by starlight, and his skin covered in small beads of water. They trailed between the defined lines of his muscles, sliding down...

He hadn't left his undershorts on like I thought he would. The water came to his hips, but it was clear from here that he was naked. And every salacious memory of how he felt between my legs poured back into my mind.

"What are you looking at, Stargirl?" he teased, and though I'd been caught staring, I didn't care.

Not tonight, with strings of freedom dancing at my fingertips.

And he'd used that name again. He'd become selective with it, only letting it slip when his guard was down.

Instead of answering immediately, I stood. The tide only came to my waist, but my hair was behind my shoulders, breasts out. "Nothing."

We remained like that for a moment, some silent dare hanging between us. *Do it*, I said with my stare. *Knock down that wall you've built.*

His eyes dropped to scan my body, his hands fisting at his sides.

Then, he backed down a step. Sank beneath the water and came back up further away from me.

Sighing, I turned away, too, and waded to the other side of the small pool. Embarrassment didn't sting like I expected. I supposed when you'd already shown someone the worst sides of you, the ones willing to lie and hurt them, there was no room left for shame.

I perched on a rock, leaning against the wall as the water lapped at my tired muscles.

"You've been here before," Cypherion said, and the husky sound of his voice shot straight to my core. He may have backed away, but he was not unaffected. He stayed halfway across the pool, though, nearly six feet separating us.

"A few times," I answered, my fingers skimming the water. "I was...busy when I lived in Valyn. Had to be available in case my mentor needed me. Apprenticing was demanding. My readings were imperative, and I was required to be behind those bars at all times."

The thought had my spine straightening. I wasn't sure when I'd started to think of the chancellor's home as a cage. When I'd lived there, it had seemed beautiful and safe.

Safe was not living, though. Safe was not free.

At some point since I traveled with Titus to Damenal, I'd

started to see the bars surrounding me and search for the views beyond them. And I thought maybe the man across the pool had something to do with it.

I was still picking apart what was unnatural about my relationship with Titus. My treatment at the Lumin Temple had been wrong. Even as a child, I recognized the uncomfortable feeling it caused in my gut, but until I met someone who made me want to defy my new mentor, I hadn't seen him as a captor at all. I'd thought him a savior.

A subtle ache went through my shoulder, breaking my thought. I rolled it to dispel the pain, likely another stiff joint from travel.

I cleared my throat. "I used to conduct sessions here." Tilting my head back, I searched the view, counting the constellations of each Angel. They were brighter here than in the mountains, in different positions in the sky.

"Did you bring other people here?" Cypherion asked.

I dropped my chin to meet his gaze.

Searing. That's how he looked at me, despite the tendrils of steam softening his features.

"Never."

The jungle's silence pressed down around us, punctured only by the soft roar of the falls and the buzz of insects, secluding us like we were the only two people on Ambrisk.

"Why do you prefer reading here?" A gentleness I'd missed filled the hollows between his words. Saying all the things he didn't.

"Readings always sit beneath my skin," I explained, holding his stare. "My magic bristles until I tap into it, sometimes painfully so. But out here, it's so quiet. It opens up room to truly listen." I pressed a hand to my chest. "The pressure sits right here, and the whispers crowd my mind, but when I dig into them it's...the purest form of ecstasy."

Cypherion's eyes darkened at that. Was there a challenge in his stare? "Is that because of your Fate ties?"

"Yes." I nodded. "Or at least I assume so. I've never been able to talk to others about how many Fates I'm aligned with." His brows drew together. "But no one has ever explained readings to me in the way I feel them."

"That must be...lonely."

I shrugged. "I didn't realize that for a while."

"What do you mean?" There was an edge to his voice now.

"I was used to feeling secluded. Used to my cages and chains, one might say. I did not see them as a problem or recognize the unnatural oppression of my desire to be close to others."

"Spirits, Vale..." Cypherion shook his head.

"I spoke to Barrett about it, actually." *Pry apart the wounds.* Let him see the person I was trying to become, and maybe he would understand. "The prince has been in chains in a way. He always accepted them because he wanted to uphold his responsibility to his people, but unlike me, Barrett saw his captors for what they were.

"He came to visit me when I was imprisoned in Damenal," I said, and Cypherion's jaw ticked. "He said some things that made me think."

"What were they?"

Had he moved closer? Surely, he was drifting around the circumference of the pool.

"Barrett told me of when he met Dax. Of how he found a light in the darkness that made him want to heal the lonely pieces and fight, to stop being complacent in his own life."

He'd said much more than that. Called me out on my lies and helped me see the pieces I'd shattered. *You can make a mosaic with broken glass,* he'd said. *All you need is determination and a new vision.*

"Is that what you've been doing? Trying to repair things? To fight?" He was only an arm's length away now, sitting on a ledge of rock with his elbows on his knees, the water to his ribs.

"I'm trying..." I took a breath. "I'm trying to fight. I haven't quite deciphered the battles. There are so many of them."

Cypherion considered that. Then, he said, "Name each one. Make them seem less shadowed."

I swallowed, my stomach turning at the thought of digging through my fears. But if I was going to do this, I wanted it to be with him.

"Valyn," I began. "The city—I don't know what we'll find there. Just stepping foot within the walls is a mountain to climb."

"Next." His voice wasn't harsh, but it was firm, directing me forward so I didn't get too caught up in one fear. Cataloging them all to make sense of it the way he always did.

He was giving me a chance, and I wouldn't be too cowardly to take it.

"Titus," I admitted. "I don't...I don't know how I feel toward him. I don't know what I'm supposed to feel about anything."

"You are not *supposed* to feel a certain way ever, Stargirl." Angels, I loved that name. It pulled me closer to him every time he said it. "There's no right or wrong when it comes to your natural response to someone. We have to work through those feelings, maybe redirect them, but how you feel is never wrong."

That was almost more confusing, trying to convince myself that however I felt was all right. It was a starting point, I supposed. And he said *we*. Did that mean he would be there while I figured it out?

No, I could not hope for that.

Still—

"You," I said.

"Me?" Cypherion's eyes widened. After a pause, he stood, wading through the waist-high water to stand before me. "What about me?"

"You're one of the battles I'm fighting." I tracked a drop of water as it slid from the curled ends of his hair and carved a path along his sculpted chest, but I swallowed and forced myself to continue. "You've been the battle I've continued to stake my heart against, trying to repair what I broke with my secrets and schemes. I want to fix it, but your intentions are murky, so it feels like another uncertain future I'm fighting."

I paused, letting those words settle between us. When he said nothing, I tilted my head back to look him in the eye. As a cave of steam formed around us, I refused to let my nerve slip. "You've built walls back up between us, and I understand why, but I've been trying to show that you can trust me. To show that I'm sincerely sorry for my choices, but also explain that I didn't understand what I was doing at the time. I still don't.

"Spirits, it's not an excuse." I shook my head. "There isn't one, but I told myself I had to let you go, and for some reason I can't."

"You told yourself what?" His voice was dark, eyes flicking between mine like he was putting pieces together.

"When we started on this journey, I told myself it was in your best interest if I let you go. If I only tried to heal what I'd broken to make amends, but not to return to...whatever it was we were before."

"And what about *your* best interest, Vale?"

I blinked up at him. "What?"

"What is it that *you* want?"

"I want..." I exhaled, the thick steam between our bodies clouding my thoughts. "I want room to breathe. I want freedom and choices and a life beyond the damn capital. I want answers, and then I want a fresh start. I want that lightness in my heart like I am precisely where I'm supposed to be, when it feels like it's expanding in my chest, not like I'm being pushed into a future because of the magic I have no control over." I paused, debating the last confession, but the words danced off the tip of my tongue. "And I want...I want *you*, Cypherion."

"Fuck, Vale." He shook his head. I'd said too much. Pushed too far and made too big of a claim. "I'm so done wanting you."

Can you feel when your heart breaks? Because I did with those words, a split, sharp and piercing and irreparable, right behind my sternum. It ached, but I collected myself around the pain.

I'd found my way out of a cage and was my own foundation. My own strength.

"Then don't." I forced myself to my feet. My breasts brushed his abs, and I almost backed down, but I had to see his expression change at the impact of what I'd say next. "Leave now if you don't want me. Please, Cypherion. Don't continue on to Valyn with me, because I *can't* do this any longer. I can't fight a battle between us while trying to hold myself together against what waits in that damn city."

My voice shook. My eyes stung.

"Vale—"

"I don't want to hear about your assignment from the Revered. I release you from it." I placed a shaking hand to his chest, tried to force him back. "You may turn off the piece of you that feels like you *have* to be here because it's your duty. Go back to your friends. I'll be fine on my own."

"You don't understand, Stargirl." His hand curled around mine, pressing it against his chest with a possessive, cementing grip. "I'm *done. Wanting. You.*"

"Then leave if you hate me so much—"

"I don't hate you, Vale."

My core throbbed at the low tone of his voice. "You don't?"

"I fear you." My stomach dropped, and both our hearts rioted, loud among the falls. "I fear how thoroughly you wrecked me and how, if I allowed you, you could do it again."

Cypherion shifted, his leg between mine, and...Fates. He was hard as steel beneath the water. He continued, "I've tried so hard to stay away from you." Spirits, he took up all the air. "Told us both I would be your friend and your guard until this was over. But it takes so much willpower to pretend I'm not still mad about you."

He said *about*. Not mad *at* me. But *about* me.

He leaned closer, pinning me against the wall, and my heart climbed further into the back of my throat with every beat. I tasted his crisp bergamot scent on the air, fresh and alluring.

"And I am so fucking tired of fighting myself," he said.

And when his lips crashed into mine, I didn't even attempt to hide the relieved gasp that slipped up my throat.

Chapter Fifteen
Vale

My back pressed up against the heated rock, and Cypherion's bare, wet skin slid against mine, heat encompassing me from every angle. His hand cupped the back of my head to stop it from slamming against the wall. The combination of that gentle thought and the way he commanded the rest of me, demonstrated that delicious care and passion he brought to everything he did.

And he kissed exactly as I remembered—like he was desperate to consume me. Lips hot and fierce as I opened for him, tongue stroking against mine both precise and firm, but hungry.

Cypherion was in complete control, and as I succumbed to him, pieces of myself that had been broken had the space to heal over. Every part of me came back to life as he kissed me deeper.

If he ever stopped again, I might crumble.

"I'm not here because it's my duty," he growled against my lips, his free hand roaming over my body and leaving chills in its wake. "I'm here because I couldn't fucking bear to let you go without me. To not know where you were or if you were okay."

"Don't leave, then," I pleaded.

And then, he was devouring me again, free hand pressing

flat to the small of my back to hold me tighter against him and thumb brushing against the curve of my waist. Even as I kissed him, that teasing stole some of my attention, and heat gathered between my thighs. The hard surfaces of his body pressed against the softer ones of mine, his grip strong and certain around me.

I ached for him, pressing closer. His cock against my stomach instead of where I wanted it was torturous.

Wrapping my arms around the back of his neck where his Bond tattoo was inked, I dug my hands into his hair. It had grown longer since I'd met him, long enough to tie back, but I loved when it was unbound like this. I took advantage now, knotting my fingers in it.

"Spirits," he breathed, moving his lips along my jaw and down my neck. "I've been telling myself for so long that I didn't want you anymore."

"Sorry to disappoint," I gasped. His hand skimmed up my ribs, calloused thumb brushing the bottom of my breast.

"I've wanted to touch you so badly, Vale," he admitted as his lips dragged over my collarbone, his voice rough. Everywhere he kissed was left in flaming goosebumps, sensations I hadn't realized were possible mingling within me.

"Touch me," I begged. "Show me."

One hand cupped my breast as he ducked his head and ran his tongue around the other nipple. He toyed with me, eyes flicking up beneath dark lashes to catch every gasp from my lips like he'd been starved without them, those blue depths dark as a midnight sky.

"Please," I breathed, hitching my leg higher around his hip to tug him to me. He was dangerously close to my center now, and Spirits, I wanted him. He nudged my entrance, and I gasped at the contact.

"You don't want me to take my time?" There was a gravelly laugh in his voice.

No, I did not want to wait tonight. I wanted to take advantage of every moment. In answer, I gripped his chin and pulled him back up to me. I kissed him harder, rolling my hips against his length and my tongue across his all at once.

"Spirits," he hissed beneath his breath, and we both looked down to where we weren't yet joined but connected.

I forgot how large he truly was, and my breath hitched. He laughed, gripping the back of my thigh with one hand and my cheek with the other, guiding my gaze up.

"Are you sure?" he asked, always so damn considerate.

I didn't want considerate tonight.

"I want you to fuck me," I told him.

"Hang on, Stargirl." And Cypherion's voice was devious like I'd never heard from him as he pushed into me. A ragged gasp fell from my lips.

"It's been a while," he groaned. "You're so tight, sweetheart."

"It's—" I breathed as he shifted his hips, my other leg wrapping around his waist. I was so full. He was everywhere, and I hadn't realized how much I missed this. "Angels."

"You can take it," he said, lips meeting my forehead and hands tightening on the backs of my thighs. Then, he thrust harder, sinking into me all the way.

For a moment we both stilled, those blue eyes exploring mine and seemingly pouring secrets between us. So many words we'd both wanted to say for months, neither of us knowing how. Things we wanted to repair, time we wanted to make up for.

This was what I'd needed. To feel cared for. To feel wanted after so long of feeling disgraced. To hear that he had not been able to abandon me like so many people had before.

His hands tightened on my legs. Cypherion pulled back slightly and slammed forward again. I clung to his shoulders, my back sliding along steam-slick rock, but he'd somehow found a surface that was smooth enough not to scrape me.

He angled my hips perfectly, and I cried out when he

reached that deeper spot inside of me that he'd been searching for. One of my hands flew up, finding a rocky ledge. My nails dug into the moss as my back arched.

"That's it," he said. His tongue flicked my nipple, biting gently. I started hurtling toward that peak as he found that spot again and again. "I remember exactly how your body responds to everything, Vale."

As if to prove it, he kept up that steady rhythm and lowered one hand between our bodies to rub tight circles on my clit. His lips skimmed up my neck, whispering beneath my ear, and I crashed into my climax.

I cried his name, and he smiled devilishly against my skin, wanting to hear it on the wind rather than kiss me through it.

Steam pillowed around us, encasing us in this escape with the stars haloed above and trees wrapping around. We were locked in our own world, trunks like bars of a cage—but this was one I had fought and clawed for.

One I would have been happy to remain in forever.

Cypherion did not follow me over that edge. He coaxed me through it, then spun and found a seat.

"What?" I asked, as he sat with me still atop him and grinned up at me.

"One more," he commanded. His voice was husky, deep and melting with the steam across my skin.

I smiled back. Resting my knees on the rock, I lifted myself up and lowered down slowly, grinding against him as he groaned. Cypherion's hands remained on my hips, steadying me but letting me take complete control.

Tendrils of his hair curled against his temples, and mine stuck to my body as I moved faster. Tangling my fingers in the hair at the nape of his neck, I leaned forward and slammed my mouth to his.

One of his hands dragged up my hip, cupping my breast. His thumb brushed across my nipple, then he pinched it. My hips jerked forward, and he settled deeper inside of me. That sly smirk he wore told me he truly remembered everything about me. About how my body reacted, about what things I liked most. Like everything we'd been and done had been plaguing his dreams as much as mine.

Cypherion matched each roll of my hips, finding every sensitive spot that had stars crashing behind my eyes.

"I've missed this," I admitted on a gasp as he gripped my ass to guide me.

"I fucking missed you," he returned. He tightened his hold like he'd never let go, and I hoped he never would again. Shaking his long hair back and looking at the rocky ledge above us, he said "Grab on, Stargirl,"

I did as he instructed, and then, he was slamming into me, both of us wild.

I cried his name a second time, and as he came, he made promises on the stars and Fates of us and never letting go again.

When we were both sated, I collapsed against him, my limbs loose and my body exhausted from finally releasing everything that had built between us. He kissed me slowly and passionately, down my arms and body. Possessive and languid.

It said everything.

I want you. I have always wanted you. I am sorry for the time we lost, but I am never letting you go again.

We sat in the springs for hours, counting the constellations above us and living in that bliss we'd stubbornly denied ourselves for too long. My head on his chest, his fingers in my hair, and our bodies and hearts entwined despite the barbed thorns of our past.

Chapter Sixteen
Cypherion

Those hot springs were some sort of Starsearcher magic, I was certain.

As I helped Vale from the water, and we forced clothes back onto our wet bodies, I wanted any excuse to stay there forever. And as we made our way to the small town we'd be staying in for the night, I was reluctant to leave that isolation, not knowing what waited for us in the capital.

"I suppose you'll be happy," Vale teased as the door to our room closed behind us. Our things were stacked neatly in the corner from when we'd stopped here earlier, but the space felt lighter. Like we'd stripped ourselves of the weighted memories we'd been dragging since Damenal.

"What?" I dragged a hand through my drying hair, tilting my head at her, a tired haze tugging at me.

Vale gestured to the room as she removed her cloak. To the two small beds on either side of the nightstand.

I barked a laugh, removing my tunic as well. Damien, I missed my leathers. "If you think there's a chance in the Spirit Realm that we aren't sharing a bed, you're going to need to ask the Fates again."

It came out like a threat, and Vale's lips quirked up at the sound.

"You seemed so inconvenienced by it before," she said, crossing her arms gracefully. Her hair dripped across her top, leaving sheer spots where it touched. Tempting.

"I was a fool." I shrugged, taking slow steps toward her. "You're not an inconvenience. Spirits, you're not a convenience either. You're so much more than that; you're fate, Vale. My fate."

Disbelief danced in her wide eyes, though, like she wasn't certain this was it. We were real, steady after battling the pain and refusals of the last few months. But the toughest battle had been avoiding her. The way she felt like she was inevitably *mine*, despite the distance I stuffed between us.

I'd been balancing on a thin line trying to keep myself away from her before she'd stripped down in the hot springs. Then, physically, she'd been irresistible. But once she'd admitted what she wanted, once I heard the damn words, there was no chance of me holding back.

Realization had slammed into me that perhaps she and I did want the same things. When she'd said that she wanted freedom from Valyn, from Titus—it was the first time I understood that maybe she didn't have to leave me.

She didn't want to be under his thumb anymore. I didn't know how we'd make that happen, but I'd figure it out for her.

Later. We would talk about all of those missed moments— unpack all the hurt and secrets so we could move forward stronger—later. We'd discuss what she wanted for the future, but right now, all *I* wanted was her between those sheets with me. And if the way her eyes were drifting closed said anything, I thought she agreed.

"Come on," I said, taking her hand and guiding her to the bed.

"I need to change," she argued.

"You seem to forget that I happen to be extremely adept at removing your clothes, Vale."

"Well, it's been so long," she said, feigning innocence. "I'll need a reminder course."

"I've been told I'm an excellent tutor."

Before she could respond, I tore off her top and skirt. Fresh marks were blooming across her collarbone and neck from where I'd been aggressive. I brushed my fingers across them, and she sucked in a breath.

"How tired are you?" I asked, partly joking, still studying those new bruises.

Mine, they said.

"More awake now." At the breathless sound of her voice, I tried to catch her eyes, but they'd dropped to where I strained against my pants, already desperate for her again.

Scooping her up, I placed her on the bed. "Something else this time," I commanded, guiding her to the pillows and working my way down her body with my mouth.

Gripping her knees, I spread them and looked down at her. "Beautiful," I praised, running two hands up her thighs. "So fucking perfect."

I wanted her to know how much I'd missed her when I was being a stubborn ass over her deceit.

Kissing the inside of her thigh, I ran two fingers over her center, gathering her wetness and circling her clit just barely. She squirmed beneath me. "As responsive as ever," I murmured into her skin.

"Hurry up," she begged.

"It's been months since I tasted you, Vale. I can't rush." I bit down softly on the inside of her thigh, her legs squeezing closed. "Are you so impatient?"

"As you said"—she was already panting—"it's been months."

I grinned, hovering my mouth in a teasingly slow pattern

down her legs. Only light kisses, not leaving anything untouched but nothing touched enough.

"A little longer won't kill you then," I said, continuing the torture.

When she was nearly bucking her hips, I pushed two fingers inside of her and finally swept my tongue over her, working into a rhythm that had her hips grinding against me and my name falling from her lips.

She'd been ravenous in the springs, and I thought it stemmed from that rejection she'd admitted. Not from me, but from so many circumstances in her life. Now, all I wanted was to remind her how fucking magnificent she was.

And as she tangled her fingers in my hair, more of that anguish I'd been living with slipped away. As I felt her skin beneath my hands, heard how I made her feel, it was like those pieces of myself I'd felt incomplete without didn't matter.

Because I had her. This. I could live without the rest, but I could not be whole without her.

I tugged her legs tighter over my shoulders, gripping beneath her ass to angle her better to my mouth. I kept up the pace with my fingers, hitting all her favorite spots and savoring each breathy sound.

"So good," Vale barely moaned, and fuck, I could come again at that sound.

She tasted like secrets exchanged under starlight—all sweet temptation and promises. I didn't know how it was possible for every inch of this girl to be starlight, but she was. Her voice, her scent, her taste. All of it was born of midnight magic.

I swirled my tongue around her clit with added pressure. A flutter around my fingers told me she was close but not quite there yet.

So, I demanded, "Let go, Stargirl," and she did, coming around my fingers and on my tongue until her limbs were limp and her breathing ragged.

I crawled back up her body and tried to prop myself on my

elbows over her, but she pulled me flush against her, taking all of my weight on her small frame, and she kissed me so deeply, I forgot where we were and every damn threat outside of this room.

Senseless. That was the word for how Vale made me. And for someone who spent every day worrying about others, senseless was a damn good place to be.

Breaking the kiss, I dropped my forehead against hers and caught my breath.

After cleaning ourselves up, Vale fell back onto the bed. "Now I'm exhausted," she said, her voice that unburdened, chiming bell again.

"Let's sleep." I stripped down to my undershorts and climbed in beside her.

"This bed is truly made for one," she joked as I made myself comfortable.

"Now it's for two," I answered, no room for argument.

Vale laughed, but I thought there was a grateful spark in her gaze. Truthfully, I felt it, too—relief at dropping that aggressive front I'd forced. She settled down against me, my arm around her, hand stroking her hip, and her head on my chest.

"I never told you this in Damenal," she began, voice already thick with sleep, "but one time I saw you in those hot springs."

"You saw me?" I asked, still drawing aimless circles against her skin.

"In a reading." Her voice was drifting further. "I didn't know it was you then. But I was maybe fifteen, and I saw you as you were when I first arrived in Damenal. Strong. In a training arena, with the friends you loved, surrounded by the power of the cypher trees."

I swallowed the weight of that confession. "Cruelty and Adoration," I muttered. We'd experienced both at each other's hands. Had the Fate been warning her? "I think I saw you," I admitted, "during my Undertaking."

Vale shot up, alert. "What?"

"During the part that challenges our emotional being," I explained, keeping it vague since I wasn't technically supposed to share anything of the ritual. "I saw you."

Vale searched my face. Those eyes. It was those olive-green eyes I saw in the Spirit Flame, a stranger then. "What do you think it means?"

I shook my head. "I don't know."

After a moment, she settled back down against me. "Maybe the Fates wanted me to find you."

In the wake of her words, her voice from the springs floated back. *You're one of the battles I'm fighting.*

Perhaps it was a useless battle on both ends, the stars always writing a story greater than us.

"Cypherion?" she mumbled.

"Yeah, Stargirl?"

"What happens when we get to the capital?" Her eyes drifted closed. "I think...I think I'm scared to be back there."

Her voice was a touch broken, vulnerability piercing through. Like what we'd done tonight had loosened the last resolve she held on her secrets, and now she was bearing them all to me. The need to reassure her was a desperate heat in my chest.

"I don't know what Valyn holds for us," I began. "But it's you and me. We'll figure it out."

"Thank you for being here." She yawned. "It makes me less afraid."

"Go to sleep, sweetheart," I said, running a hand down her back and resting my cheek on her head. "I'll be here in the morning."

CHAPTER SEVENTEEN
CYPHERION

"It's been six years, I think, since I was in Valyn," I said as Erini's steady stroll carried us through the narrow jungle path. Ahead, the towering trees were thinning, and I could almost make out the white-washed stone comprising the walls of the capital.

"Six years," Vale mused. "It probably hasn't changed too much, then."

I ducked beneath a low hanging vine, eyes on her. "I remember it being sprawling. Eleven districts, right? And each has a contributing Capital Council member who reports to Titus?"

"It appears you *do* do your research." She looked over her shoulder, brows up and a teasing smile on her lips. Good. I wanted to keep her smiling throughout this.

Hopefully, we'd get into the city, find the archives and whatever information they held for her sessions, and leave without trouble.

"Knowing what I'm facing," I said, casually, "what the world is made of, makes everything seem more approachable."

"That it does." Vale's voice shrank, uncertain, my hope of easing this journey for her withering with it. "Whereas the coastal cities and those bordering the lakes are built into the hill-sides and cliffs, Valyn commands the land. The city is bordered by a high wall and magic thrives within."

"Because Valyrie lived here?" Much like Damenal was Damien's founding capital, Valyn was the home to the Starsearcher Angel.

Vale nodded. "Her legacy left the land powerful."

"A likely place for a treasure to be stored," I commented.

Of all the places in Starsearcher Territory, a city blessed with magic and important to their Prime Warrior was the most likely to hide her emblem.

But we had to focus on Vale's disrupted power first.

I chose my next words carefully. "Do you think a part of you would feel more secure if we went to Titus's manor?"

Vale's eyes snapped to mine, a crease between her brows. "Why?"

"Maybe then you'd have more control over the situation." I shrugged, holding her stare as Erini stepped through the last line of jungle foliage and Valyn unspooled ahead of us. "You can write the script to this encounter, Vale. If he does find out we're here, would it not feel better if you dictated how and when?"

She considered, gazing toward the city gates. Had she spent time in this area? Did she have memories here?

Even with the walls broken down between us, there were still things I couldn't pick apart. Pieces I was relearning as her secrets shed new light on all sides of her.

Though clearly things had changed between us last night, and I meant every word I'd said—I wasn't going to hold back anymore—we wouldn't heal because of one moment. That distance I'd nurtured between us sprouted roots that clawed through the soil of whatever we were. We had to dig them up.

"Come here," I said, dismounting Erini and helping Vale off Marage. Her hands stayed on my arms, eyes on me—not the gleaming silver gates in the distance. "You don't have to do anything you don't want to. If you'd like to spend the entire time here with hoods drawn and knives at the ready, I gladly will." I brushed a strand of hair behind her ear, cupping her jaw. "Whatever makes you comfortable, Stargirl."

Vale sighed, relaxing into me with a touch of hesitancy, like she almost couldn't believe my words. After the way Titus had convinced her he cared for her and then abandoned her, I wasn't surprised.

Her hands snaked behind my neck, trembling slightly, and her head fell against my chest. "I'd like to leave this city and all its fated tales behind."

I rubbed circles on her back, my stare locked on the silver ink etched across her shoulder. "Then that's what we'll do."

~

"THE ARCHIVES we need are in the second district," Vale explained, her spine as stiff as her words.

It made my jaw grind to see this timid side of her. It was similar to the person she'd projected when she first arrived in Damenal. Meek on the orders of Titus. Fingers fidgeting with her appearance.

I did my best to shove aside my frustration, ignoring the way my hands itched for a fight, and asked, "Which are we in now?"

"The fourth," she said. "This area is primarily food markets and taverns, so I thought we could find a place to rest and pick up whatever we may need."

The gray cobblestones beneath our feet were dusted with scraps from the surrounding tenants, tents pouring into the street outside storefronts. The buildings lining the walkways were rough white stone, coated from centuries of dirt that proved they'd seen age-old stories. Thin metal balconies lined the second floors, many of the small shops on this street hosting apartments above. And from those, greenery dotted with tiny white, pale blue, and purple flowers draped over the edge, the night-blooming buds closed to the daylight.

We guided our horses through the narrow stalls, our voices drowned by the shouts of tellers and customers alike. But the beauty of this new city was lost on me as Vale cast a furtive look over her shoulder, awaiting my answer.

And protectiveness mounted in my blood.

"That's a great idea," I said through a tight throat. "Wherever you think is best."

I followed Vale with our hoods drawn and tried to see this city through the various stages of her life.

I tried to imagine it as a child who'd been rescued from a temple. Were the crowds overwhelming? Perhaps she'd clung to the safety of the chancellor's manor at first.

Maybe once she'd been allowed to explore the winding streets, she indulged in the herbs being chopped on one corner or the decadent smell of garlic roasting at the tavern nearby.

Or had she gone to the silk merchant as a teenager, shopping for her favorite skirts on the few days she was granted leave?

Did she see other warriors her age completing lessons or lounging outside the sweet shop and feel alone? My heart clenched at that thought, and the entire city soured.

As we passed a warrior with an intricate layer of ink winding up his arm and to his jaw, I only saw the silver tattoo across her brand.

When we peeked in a tent clouded with incense down an alley, I saw a girl whose magic isolated her among her peers.

And rather than the home I'd expected this city to be for her, it all felt cold and lonely.

Chapter Eighteen
Vale

My magic pressed against my skin the moment we entered Valyn.

It had been mounting, insistent, ever since we returned to the territory, but as Cypherion and I journeyed through the capital, the Fates whispered even more. Nine voices mingled through my being, their need to release a pressure against my chest.

"How do you want to go about this?" Cypherion asked, sinking into a chair at the rickety table in the room we'd rented above a candle shop.

It was off the main road, not one of the more frequented boutiques that spotted the market districts. One of my favorites I'd ever visited, though those were few.

The owners told me years ago that they rented space in the attic to travelers, but didn't hang a sign out front to avoid a rowdy crowd. It was the only place I recalled, and I'd been hoping to Valyrie that it was available.

With my hood up, I didn't think the woman downstairs recognized me, but I remembered the gentle lines framing her lips and eyes, the signs of someone who lived a long life and smiled plenty during it.

Instantly, safety wrapped around me.

But once we closed the door to the attic, a stifling feeling ground against my sternum, only adding to the magic pounding through me. There was one small bed and a basin to wash in, not much other furniture crowding the space, but the aromatic fragrances wafting through the floorboards from the candles below stole the fresh air.

Fingers twitching, I leaned across the table to throw open the singular small round window in the room and inhaled the scent of Valyn's clear skies and flowers. Afternoon sunlight streamed through the dust in the rafters, and I chewed my lip as I peeked out over the wooden shutters and tiled roofs of the city.

My city.

No.

No longer my city. Had it ever been?

I'd never truly explored the buildings draped across the hilly Starsearcher land, nor the woven pathways and what lingered in the shadows. I'd only visited a few establishments, and those were on a regimented schedule.

I didn't know Valyn the way others knew their homes. Not the way Cypherion knew Damenal. Memories of wandering hidden alleys and shops with him rang through my mind, his explanations on each one thorough.

Cities were not just fixtures and buildings and shops, as I'd thought. They held secrets buried within their corners, adventures beneath the cobblestones.

What tavern was the best for dancing?

What market had the freshest produce?

What shows or gambling halls or fighting dens could one only venture into with a known password?

I knew none of those answers about Valyn, had only viewed the city as it pertained to my magic. Where to study, where to worship, and where to purchase supplies when I was allowed to do so myself. I'd thought that's all there was to it.

Since we'd reentered, though, my magic strained against my skin. The tattooed brand beat with a beckoning instinct. It wanted out—all of it.

The need to read was a tingling allure that I suppressed, and as I gazed out over Valyn, my mind couldn't help but highlight each temple I knew of, like they were summoning me to convene with the Fates.

"Stargirl?"

A sure but soft voice brought me back to myself. A gentle grip on my wrist and the strum of a thumb across my pulse.

I snapped my eyes down to Cypherion's, worry gazing back among the deep blues.

"Talk to me," he said.

"I..." I cast one more glance over the city, then turned my back on the window and stepped between his legs. Cypherion kept one hand on mine, the other resting gently against my hip.

"Tonight, we should go to the Second District and visit the temple. See what sort of protection is around the archives. It's been years since I've visited that location, and I'm not sure what their current system is."

His brows pulled together, clearly suspicious of my obvious discomfort. But I avoided his eyes and stifled the magic riling within me.

"We should wear our cloaks and hide what weapons we can beneath them." I looked at the sword Ophelia had given me when we first left Damenal, now resting beside Cypherion's scythe. Warmth gathered in my chest at the sight. "We don't want to look like a threat."

He scoffed, and that had a small smile breaking on my lips. I looked down at him, the warrior with a heart as soft as an Angel's wing but who commanded weapons with the brutality of the gods.

A complexity, a duality.

Mine.

And some of that discomfort cleared further. In this room,

with him, I was safe but not caged. I was freer than I'd ever been, the future retained more promise than even my magic could guarantee, but it was mine to wield.

I lifted my hand to the back of his neck and curled his hair around my fingers. "How are you feeling?"

For a moment, he seemed surprised that I asked. His head tilting slightly, considering—and he finally admitted, "I'm worried."

"About the archives?"

"Yes," he said, gently massaging my hip through the chiffon of my skirt. "But also my friends."

"When was the last you heard from them?" They'd been keeping communication scarce, but it was clear from the strain of his voice how much it pained him to be away from them.

"Ophelia wrote a few days ago that they're stationary for now, so my letters can be more frequent and contain more detail, as they'll be less likely to arrive at the wrong location, but they're still being vague since you and I are traveling." He huffed a laugh. "Except Tolek. He sent me three pages describing every hand he won in cards and every tavern he wanted to show me when we join them."

"Soon," I promised, tracing his soft smile lightly.

"Hopefully, yeah." He sighed.

"Do you know where they are?"

"Somewhere in the Western Outposts." He shrugged, but held tighter to me. "They said they would send more information once we were done traveling."

I brushed my fingers down the back of his neck. "Can you feel them through your tattoo?"

Cypherion lifted a hand, meeting mine and dragging his fingers over the thin outline of mountains. "The Bond is like a net that casts us back toward the mountains to fulfill our purpose after the Undertaking. And every Mystique that has one can feel that connection." He dropped his hand, shaking his head. "But we're all individual strings making up the whole. It's hard to differentiate one from the other."

"I understand." I absently ghosted my hand over the tattoo on my shoulder. The one that did not hold the same magic as Mystiques but was powerful enough to release me from any oaths held to Lumin Temple.

Cypherion's eyes narrowed for a moment, then his expression softened as his mind worked down whatever path it was set on.

"I never asked." He paused, cheeks slightly flushing. "Do Starsearchers have a form of commitment like the Bind?"

"We exchange vows in a ceremony," I explained. "Incense is burned, a joint reading done. Then, and only if the Fates deem it appropriate, some searchers receive commitment tattoos. Become Fatesworn. But I've never seen it done."

"The Fates have to give permission?"

I nodded. "They don't choose whom you end up with—except in rare legends—and if they don't approve you do not *have* to heed their warnings for the first part of the ritual, but you can't receive any tattoos without that recognition."

"Different," he said. "The Bind is all about choice, not permission."

I shrugged. "They're both beautiful in their own way. One about freedom, one about a promise of the stars."

Unspoken questions weighed the air between us. Could one receive both? Could tattoos be exchanged outside of clans? What would the Fates think?

Neither of us voiced those curiosities, though. And I thought we were both okay with that. With reigniting whatever we'd had before Daminius and easing back into it.

We did not need the approval of the Fates.

I spun my oldest tarnished ring around my finger as I considered it, and Cypherion tracked the movement.

"You've worn that much longer than the others." It wasn't a question, but he opened the opportunity for me.

"It was my mother's," I said, staring at the opal set in the center. "She gave it to me before..." I didn't finish the sentence, but he understood. "She gave one to me and one to my sister when we were young. We wore them on chains around our necks until they fit—or, I did. I like to imagine she did, too. That she's out in the world somewhere with a twin ring to mine."

I'd told him about my sister before—what I remembered of her. How fiercely protective she was.

"Have you ever considered looking for her?" he asked, gently.

I shook my head. "I didn't want to seek them out, take them from whatever comfortable lives they may have forged for themselves after I was stolen. If their magic is anything like mine..."

"It would be used like yours, too."

I nodded, swallowing that fear. Cold dripped through my veins like I imagined the heart of the most vengeful Fate felt.

"You don't think they know where you are? That you became Titus's apprentice?"

"They couldn't," I explained. Nerves fluttered through me. "I shortened my name when I was still living at the temple."

"*What?*"

"Harlen started calling me Vale, but my true name is Adelline, my middle name Valencia." I curled a strand of his hair around my finger. "It's not a huge jump, but I was only ever Adelline Valencia to my parents and sister, and Titus never made my family name public knowledge—thank the Fates."

"Adelline Valencia," Cypherion said, testing it. He searched my face. "It's beautiful. So are you. But I like Vale."

"I do, too."

And if it kept my family protected, I'd never answer to my true name again.

My eyes stung, but I blinked away the tears, clenching my hand with the opal stone of my mother's ring facing my palm.

"Why don't you write to your friends?" I suggested. "Tell them where we are and give them an update on our plan."

"Yeah," Cypherion said slowly, both of us trying to focus on the present conflicts again. As he reached for his pack, I moved to step away, but his voice cut through the room. "Where are you going?"

A tug on my wrist, and I was falling into his lap with a small squeal, all my mourning from a moment before vanishing with his warmth around me.

"Giving you space?" My words turned up at the end, because what in the Fates did he mean?

Cypherion dumped his supplies on the table, the corked inkwell rolling. "Write the letter with me?"

There was a new vulnerability to his words. An invitation to stand together as we presented new findings and strategies to his friends—his friends that were not only the current leaders of the Mystique Warriors, but a group of individuals who comprised the deepest parts of his heart. The ones he'd fought and sacrificed for. The ones he would risk his life for.

Cypherion raised his brows hesitantly, asking me to be a part of this with him, his care for them bleeding out between us.

I would bottle up that worry for him, widen the room to make space for everything he felt and feared.

"Of course," I whispered.

And as he sighed, the weight of our mission fell on me again. Yes, this was about untangling my magic, but the implications stretched so much further than that. They extended past the archives, past the walls of this capital, clear across the continent.

They were pressing down on those Cypherion loved most, and though he didn't say it, I thought he was afraid of what the end would bring.

He shouldn't have to carry those fears alone. He wouldn't anymore.

This started with *my* magic, and I would do whatever was within my power to help him.

CHAPTER NINETEEN
VALE

"MOST TEMPLES ARE FOR WORSHIP AND READING, with the academies attached to them for residents," I explained to Cypherion for what must have been the tenth time, though he kept listening attentively.

We strolled as casually as we could through the Second District and toward the largest temple in the capital, which sat above the archives. With the sun having set, some of the less savory parts of Valyn were waking. Nearly every open window emitted puffs of pastel smoke that I did my best to avoid.

It was likely only recreational—not the kind that would trigger a reading—but I didn't want to find out.

"But there will be guards," Cypherion said.

As a group of warriors pushed past us, he placed his hand to my lower back, keeping me close. I tried not to look at any of them, didn't want them peering beneath my hood on the off chance that they remembered the chancellor's apprentice. Instead, I ducked my head and leaned into Cypherion.

Spirits, being so hidden was strange, but in a way, it awarded a new level of freedom. I didn't have to be looking over my shoulder every moment. Didn't have to worry that I'd be recognized so easily. And given that it was winter, it wasn't suspicious of us to be so concealed.

I answered Cypherion as that group drifted further down the street, "There are guards, but they're employed by the temples and academies. Everyone who grows up at a temple, or is hired by them, is trained." I was. "They're usually unpracticed in real combat—the ones who didn't join the armies against Kakias at least—but it's best if we can avoid them."

I didn't want to harm innocent Starsearchers. If these guards were like most, Cypherion would destroy them in a battle.

He hummed in agreement, and we continued on. Finally, at the end of a wide street, the temple's looming silhouette rose into the night.

We stopped at the base of the stairs, the elaborate carved stone facade glaring down at us, pointed towers and stained glass adorning the sacred space.

"Weapons?" Cypherion asked to distract me, craning his neck to see the top of the spires glinting in the moonlight.

Beneath my cloak, my triple blades were heavy in my weapon belt. The extra knives Cypherion insisted I slide into sheaths on my thighs and wrist chilled me through the leather.

"They'll have them," I muttered.

For a moment, my chest tugged. Swirls of murky blues and bursts of bright whites pressed against my mind. Fates whispered in my ears.

Fatecatcher, one roared.

But just as quickly, they were gone.

And we were left staring at gray stone and twelve large, arched windows. Candles flickered behind eleven, depicting a pivotal story of each Fate.

With a nod at those windows, Cypherion extended a hand to lead me up the steps and said, "Let's go see what they hold, Stargirl."

As I marched up those stairs, his boots echoing on stone

behind mine, comfort wrapped itself around my bones and made each step easier. Cypherion wasn't leaving me. Together, we would decipher what hid inside.

The domed center of the temple looked down at us as we entered. Stained glass in the rounded skylights melted the stars so they swam in the deep navy, a few propped open to view the constellations. A balcony lined the ceiling, telescopes poking out, exactly as our Angel liked to practice.

With each step inside, magic fluttered quicker beneath my skin.

Benches lined the center aisle up to the altar, a few Starsearchers kneeling between them. A handful of guards lined the walkway, but no one noticed us.

Alcoves brimmed with incense around the edge of the main hall. Curtains were pulled closed on every one, waiting for deeper readings to be conducted and candles flickered within. Twelve spaces in total. One for each Fate.

Like the windows, the one at the end remained dark.

And halfway down the left wall, a wooden door cut between two of them.

"This way," I whispered.

Cypherion said nothing, but the tension rolling off his shoulders was palpable, the ticking of his jaw nearly audible. He was likely counting each of the knives strapped to his person, planning the quickest exit.

The skylights cast pockets of moonlight onto the tile as we made our way through the temple to that wooden door. Our breaths were loud, and my fingers jittered at my sides.

Silently, Cypherion slipped his hand into mine, steadying me.

As we reached the door, my heart sank. "A lock," I whispered.

Of course the archives were unlocked to only the acolytes. What had I been expecting? Just because every door had appeared open to me before—when I came on Titus's orders—did not mean they were still.

Cypherion draped his hand around my shoulder and pretended to admire the statues of ancient warriors standing on either side of the door.

"Sealed magically or with a key?" he mumbled.

I mimicked his nonchalance despite the combination of nerves and magic bubbling within me, slipping my arm around his waist. But I looked out of the corner of my eye to the metal lock. It appeared simple, a keyhole in the center.

"It's basic," I said.

"Good," Cypherion whispered. "There's only one guard on this side of the temple." He tilted his head to the right. "Go ask him for assistance with the candles in one of these alcoves, and when you're done, meet me behind that door."

I looked up to him, my brows pulling together, but he kissed my temple softly and sent me on my way.

"Excuse me, sir?" I asked, keeping my hood pulled up but ensuring my tone was light. The guard turned to me curiously, dark-blond hair swaying around his shoulders. "I'd like to use one of the private alcoves, but I can't seem to locate the matches."

"Sorry about that, Miss," he said, nodding. "I'll go fetch some."

I watched him leave, and fought every instinct to check on Cypherion. Instead, I drifted to the end of the benches lining the main aisle and stared up at the dome. At the heavens stretching beyond, whirling with star-kept secrets.

What is it you plan for us?

Silence hung around me as I waited for an answer. But the Fates only continued to stir wickedly within my mind, strumming along my veins, like a poetic melody. Giving no answers.

"Here you are," the guard said, returning with a long rectangular box. "May the stars guide you."

"Thank you." With a demure nod, I disappeared into the

nearest alcove and pulled the curtain, leaving a gap to watch him retreat. I lit the candles but not the incense. Not until he was far enough away.

Only then did I ignite the smoky haze, filling the space to give the illusion that I was reading within, and slip out before it could take me.

I scampered quietly back up the aisle, clinging to shadows. The door to the archives was unlocked.

As I tugged it softly against the jam behind me, strong arms wrapped around my waist. I gasped, but that bergamot scent had me sighing. I held tight to his wrists as I craned my neck, his blue eyes shining beneath his hood.

"I wasn't aware lock picking was on your list of skills," I whispered.

"I have a wealth of talents you've yet to see, Stargirl."

Though nerves still jittered through me, I laughed softly.

Peeking around him, I nodded down the corridor. "That staircase leads down to the archives."

"Ninth level," Cypherion said, checking over his shoulder. "Let's go."

We descended, low-ceilinged chambers crammed with stacks of books waiting on each floor. Offices, tutoring rooms, and session halls branched off the aisles. Despite the chill above ground, mystlight kept the archives comfortable for the long nights that acolytes worked or read. As students of the temple above us, they lived in the attached dormitories and were required to attend an absurd number of lessons, sessions, and trainings, making nights the best time to study.

Fires flickered in grates, scholars and warriors lining each floor, chatting, reading, and working. No one even thought to look twice at us, and we did not care to disturb them. If my magic wasn't straining so aggressively to be used, I might have liked it here.

But the pounding of the Fates intensified the deeper we got, spiraling down that staircase in the center of the archives.

Until we reached the sixth level down.

When I looked around the curved stone corner, my gaze caught on an office door at the end of the first aisle.

On the words etched possessively into the wood.

Chancellor Titus Verian.

"Chancellor?" I muttered.

"What's that?" Cypherion said, reaching for a weapon as he spun. His eyes narrowed on the plaque, and he immediately stepped to block me from view of anyone on this floor.

When he spoke again, his voice was darker than before. "He has a study here?"

"I...didn't know..."

I didn't know.

I was Titus's apprentice, supposedly the only student he saw as worthy of holding that position. I attended Capital Council meetings with him, conducted readings at his request, and yet...

I had not known of this office in the archive temple.

Disappointment and abandonment crashed over me in icy waves. The worst was the shock, though. Because I shouldn't have expected anything else.

It sliced through me like each letter on the door was being carved into my skin.

"Vale?" Gently, Cypherion reached for my hand.

The stairs to the lower archive levels were just behind us. Only three more. I should get to the ninth level so we could leave.

But I couldn't stop whatever force pulled me toward the door, dragging Cypherion down the aisle behind me. Couldn't resist as my hand raised and drifted across the letters spelling out his name and title.

Father. Captor.

Savior. Ruler.

Liar—

No.

Heat flared through my shoulder.

Titus was good. He *was*. He had to be. Titus had saved me sixteen years ago, and if he had not written to me since Daminius, there was a reason. A valid explanation, I was certain.

That mantra played on a hypnotic loop through my mind as magic continued to pound beneath my skin. As that tangle of wild stars begged to be released.

Flashes of light and wings and falling constellations. Images of legends and gods and locked cages.

Footsteps echoed down the nearest aisle, coming toward us.

"Come on, Vale," Cypherion said, his hand squeezing mine.

But my feet remained rooted to the tile. "Titus..."

He was the one I was supposed to be working for. He was the one who had rescued me from that temple as a child, who had seen promise in me that no one else had.

They all wanted to use my magic, but Titus nurtured it. Power danced within my veins at the reminder.

That burning was back along my shoulder and nine midnights eddied through my mind. The footsteps were getting closer, laughter with them now.

"Vale, we have to go."

"No...Titus..."

"Enough of him, dammit."

The swirling pressure crescendoed in my mind, stars popping along my vision. My shoulder flared, and strong arms hoisted me from the ground, fleeing the temple.

CHAPTER TWENTY
CYPHERION

Vale didn't speak the entire walk back to the candle shop.

She kept her head down and hood up as we climbed the stairs to our room and quietly slipped off our weapons and cloaks. It wasn't a tense silence, but it was the kind that bristled against my skin nonetheless. The kind that seemed to heighten every other sound besides the ones you needed to hear most.

I waited as Vale slipped into a nightgown and dumped her clothing on the floor rather than folding it as she usually would. She drifted to the lone window in the room and looked out over the city. I remained beside the mantle, one hand on the wood, fingers drumming in a slow measure to try to steady myself.

When I couldn't take the stillness anymore, I picked up her clothes and folded them, then started arranging each of our weapons, polishing those that had gotten scuffed after days of travel.

But still, a beast roared within my chest. It lifted its head and breathed hot fire at the way the chancellor's name on the door had frozen Vale in the archives.

As I carefully laid her triple blades on the shelf, I remembered how her fingers had reached for the wood. How her voice had been so shocked and betrayed.

I...didn't know...

It was only an office, but to her it was an entire world shattering. Every star in the sky breaking.

It was another abandonment, twisting a blade that was plunged between her ribs months ago.

She wanted in. She wanted to patch that wound and cleanse the knife herself.

And that made my stomach churn.

I aligned the last blade and glanced over my shoulder. Still, she stood before that window. The roaring in my head mounted.

I told it to quiet, because it was clear whatever had been cracking within my Stargirl for months had firmly crumbled tonight. A severance of some pivotal piece of her spirit.

"Vale..." I said slowly, coming to stand beside her.

"Hm?" she hummed, eyes glued to the city.

But they weren't still.

Her gaze roved over each sculpted building, stained glass, and spire, as if searching for what else she may have missed.

Slowly, I leaned my shoulder against the wall beside the window and crossed my arms, not obscuring the view but hoping to catch her eye. "What happened back there?"

"It was just acolytes," she said, brushing me off with a slow tilt of her head. "Next time, we should hide among the shelves. We should have tonight. Then we could be done."

Her voice was like something from a dream, higher than usual and floating around us. Not at all grounded or logical.

"Before the acolytes, Vale," I said. "What happened to you?"

Finally, she met my eyes.

And a scarred spirit stared back through those olive-green irises, so dim and full of surrender.

"His name was on the door," she whispered.

"I saw it." I nodded for her to continue.

"And I did not know he had an office in the temple." Her fingers gripped the edge of her nightgown, crumpling the silk. "I was his apprentice; I was the student he trusted most"—her voice cracked—"and saw the most promise in. And I did not know."

"Vale..." I took in the shadows in her eyes and the frantic grasp of her hands to just hold on to *something*. Something solid, something real. "Why are you so loyal to him still?"

I didn't know if either of us were ready to have the conversation, but I'd lead her there and hold her through it if she wanted to try.

"Because I have to be."

"You don't," I whispered, shaking my head.

"I do." Her hand flashed to her shoulder, where that tattoo gleamed in silver ink.

"Just because he saved you once doesn't mean he's incapable of putting chains around your wrists again, Stargirl."

"No, he didn't." She shook her head, retreating as if the window was suddenly a cliff's edge she teetered over. "Titus is g-good. Titus wants the best for me."

Again, she clutched at her tattoo, pain twisting her face.

Anger ripped through me to see her like this, to witness everything she thought she knew being overturned, clinging to the beliefs planted in her mind. I swallowed the rage that burned up my throat and tried my hardest to focus on her trembling hands and sharp breaths. To not let my frustration out.

"Maybe, it's time we talk about the possibility that he doesn't want what he's claimed, Vale. That he has other motives—"

"He gave me *everything*," she snapped, fists tightening. "I am only *here* because he pulled me out of Lumin sixteen years ago!"

"Only to stick you in another cage!" I said, much more aggressively than I intended. The jaws of my anger opened wider, finally letting loose all the thoughts I'd kept behind barbed teeth. "Titus has manipulated you for years, Vale! He's used you—why? He's had you scheming and lying for him, risking *lives* for his secrets, and what did he do when you needed him?"

Her jaw ticked, lips pressing tight together, and one hand still clawing at her shoulder. But we couldn't keep dancing around this, not when the slightest push had toppled her resolve.

No matter how badly it hurt us both to shove her into this truth.

"What did he do when the secret came out and Ophelia and I tried to make you a prisoner?"

"He saved me," she muttered, barely opening her lips to speak. Like if she did, she'd free fall over the edge of the cliff, the truth weighing her down and stealing every shred of control.

I drove her toward that drop.

"*What did he do, Vale?*"

"HE LEFT ME!" she shouted, chest heaving. "He—he left me."

It didn't feel good to hear. To see the acceptance shattering across her face, her body, like her bones were fracturing. It had been a different sort of cage holding her up, one she'd formed within herself around her captor's manipulation.

It was the base of her. And now, as it rippled across her features, as her shaking hands dragged through her hair and tangled at the roots, trying to grasp onto one steady thing in reality, she free fell into the loss.

"He left me," she repeated, voice so small. No hint of the starlight that burned through her veins or the strength I loved so fucking much. "Not one letter. I wrote to him every week, begging him to negotiate with Ophelia, to get me out of that prison."

Ophelia. *And me.*

I'd been as complicit in Vale's pain as the chancellor. The

realization was sour in the back of my throat, a stampede of warrior horses pounding through my chest.

"I just wanted him to help me. I just needed help...help. I needed him to care." Her words were rushed, eyes stuck to the floor. "I needed him to care like he told me he did. I needed him to be a mentor like he said he was."

Her knuckles went white as she tugged on her hair, knees buckling. I raced forward, catching her around the waist. Vale's eyes flashed up to mine, teary and wrecked. They widened, like she'd only just remembered I was there.

Then, her hands gripped my arms, and she was talking *to* me again.

"He swore to me when he took me from the temple that life was going to be better. And it *was*. It was so much better here, but it was just another chain around my neck. By covering the brand, he was only making me beholden to him."

I nodded, swallowing past the thickness in my throat. "Not all motives are innocent. Sometimes, a gesture that seems good-natured can have expectations weighing it down."

Her nails dug into my skin, but I let her use me to ground herself. I'd bleed out before her if it was what she needed now.

"I don't think he ever loved me," Vale admitted. I thought she might have been considering it for a while, maybe even knew it for sure, but hadn't wanted to say it out loud. Today, though, after the archives and the discovery of his secret office, after the feel of this city against her skin and the memories it pushed forward, she finally did.

"You should not have to guess if someone loves you," I said.

"The last time I knew love was when I was four. I barely remember how that felt, it's just a haze of memories." The tears stopped falling, her gaze turning more thoughtful and desperate as she sought mine. "I saw it when I came to Damenal, though."

"Tolek and Ophelia—"

"You, Cypherion." She squeezed my arms, easing her clawing grip. An emptiness settled in me. I wanted it back.

Wanted her marks on my skin to remind us both that I was here with her through whatever she might face. "The way you love your friends...it's deep. It's true and unquestioning. That's the kind of love that would never die."

The kind she wanted.

The kind I wanted to give her.

I swore to Damien I'd show it all to her.

"I'm sorry," I said, "for the part I played in your imprisonment. For not trying to see past my own selfish pain and understand what he was doing sooner."

"Pain isn't selfish," Vale corrected. She was fully supporting her own weight now, but still we stayed entwined, her body against mine, so every breath pressed her tighter. "It can turn us rotten, certainly, but to feel hurt is not a selfish act."

"I indulged it. Used it as a guard and kept you away because it was easier than exploring the alternative."

"I hurt you," she tried to justify, her voice kicking up with a hint of stubborn argument.

"And I added to your pain," I shot back. Spirits, were we really going to argue over who hurt the other more? Who deserved to feel more guilty? "The details of it don't matter. We're here. Together. And Titus is never going to slip that chain back around your neck."

She stiffened at his name. I ran a hand down her spine, the other cupping her cheek.

"He left me," she repeated, but there was more clarity in her gaze now.

"I'm so sorry he did that." I pressed a kiss to her forehead. "It's not a reflection of you, your magic, or your worth." Pulling back, I swiped away the tears streaking down her cheeks. "You are worth so much more than someone who leaves you, Stargirl. You outshine every damn star in the sky, outweigh every Fate."

"I don't know what comes next for me without him."

"Do you still want to go back?" My heart stuttered.

But she shook her head. "I don't think I can."

Relief loosened my chest. "None of us truly know where we're going."

"But I'm his—"

"You don't belong to anyone, Vale," I said, quickly shutting her down. "You are your own warrior, your own Starsearcher. Powerful enough that the chancellor wanted your magic at his disposal. You can defy any ruler, any fate written." And I would help her do it. "I would do horrible things before I let him take you back," I promised, ducking to kiss her and seal that vow between us.

Vale deserved freedom. She deserved to understand the tangles of her own power and embrace it.

And even if it meant I plunged a blade through the Starsearcher Chancellor's chest, I would see that she won it.

Chapter Twenty-One
Vale

My bones were wrung out when I woke the next morning, but Cypherion's arms kept me tight against him, holding me together.

I laid there in the dawn, lulled by the even rise and fall of his chest under my head. My eyes were swollen despite Cypherion making me wash my face with cold water once I stopped crying last night. A hollow had formed within my chest when I'd finally cracked, fissures stretching from its delicate edges through the rest of my body. Down to the marrow of my bones and the wisps of my spirit—something had broken.

But I studied the sun streaking through the window and illuminating specks of dust in the air, and I realized that I didn't feel as aimless as those wandering particles.

I expected the ache to weigh me down. To make moving on seem a mountainous task in the face of realizing how many lies I'd been fed. The questions still swarmed within me.

What was in that office?

Why did Titus keep secrets?

Why did he keep me?

But instead of sinking into the dark cavern, my magic tingled beneath my skin. It called to me, bolstered me.

There was a hollow in me. One yawning to swallow everything I knew, unrepentant and leaving nothing behind. But the deepest voids between the stars held a refracted beauty. A lack of light that allowed one to exist with the secrets one didn't want to face.

The ones I never would have chosen to conquer if I'd remained within my cage.

Those bars had been blown wide open, my future with them. And though I had so many questions, I wanted to explore what lurked where the stars broke.

Cypherion stirred, his arms tightening around me. "Good morning, Stargirl," he mumbled, his voice thick with sleep.

"Good morning." I rolled onto my stomach to face him. Reluctantly, he loosened his grip but kept one hand across my back, drawing slow circles along my spine, but he didn't open his eyes. "Still not a morning person?"

Cypherion was always the first to arrive at training when we were in Damenal, but no one else saw how he had to drag himself out of bed and dunk his face in cold water to wake himself up for the day.

He groaned. "I like the morning well enough. I don't like the waking up part much. Especially not when it means you're getting out of my bed."

I laughed softly, and finally, he cracked one eye open. Confusion unfurled in his stare, waking him fully as last night came back to him.

"How are you?" he asked, propping himself on an elbow and evaluating me.

"I'm okay," I said. When he gave me a skeptical look, I added, "I truly am. I don't have the answers, yet, but I feel as if I've accepted the truth."

"Acceptance is a good place to start." Absently, he smoothed his fingers up my spine. "What do you want to do now?"

"What do you mean?" I cocked my head.

Something softened behind his eyes. Not pity, but unease. "We can leave, Vale."

"We can't—"

He pushed himself upright, leaning against the headboard. "If it's too hard or too risky for you to be here, we can leave. Go back to Ophelia and everyone and figure out some other way to restore your readings and get the answers we need."

"I won't be selfish or afraid of my magic," I said, sitting up and crossing my legs. "I want to help Ophelia find these emblems if I can, and I want to get answers about my own power."

I was tired of being in the dark.

A small smile quirked on Cypherion's lips at my determination. "Then we'll get them. How, though? Last night..."

I shook my head, at a loss for an explanation. I hadn't just frozen when I saw Titus's office—I'd shattered. There was some sort of pull from me to be there. To see him.

"I don't know what that was, but we'll avoid the sixth level when we return. I know it's there now. I can prepare myself mentally, and..."

"And?" he asked when I paused.

I blew out a breath, but wings of anticipation fluttered in my chest. "And I think I'll need to read. Or at least attempt it." Cypherion opened his mouth to argue, eyes growing defensive, but I continued, "I've been avoiding it for too long."

"Remember what happened in the Labyrinth and Seawatcher Territory when you conducted sessions." A hint of desperation pierced his voice, those memories flashing between both of us. "Or at the fighting ring when you weren't even trying to read."

"Maybe I need to stop suppressing it," I suggested, leaning forward and taking his hand. "My magic has been more insistent since we've been in Valyn. It's been calling to me, begging me to use it, and if I don't let it out soon, I fear I'll lose that battle."

And it was the use of that word that broke through to him. *Fear.* Because Cypherion lived to protect those he cared about.

"You didn't mention," he said, concern weighing his gaze as it dragged across my body again, like he could target that power and rescue me from any pain it may cause.

"I was trying to avoid it." I shrugged. Goosebumps peppered my skin at the Fate ties stirring within me, voices attempting to call me. I shoved them down to finish explaining, my voice soft. "I've always embraced my magic before, never stifled it. I thought I could ignore it this time, but last night proves I can't run from everything."

Cypherion's hand tightened around mine. "And you think a session will fix something?"

I nodded. "Reading has always been the answer for me. When I need guidance, I turn to the Fates."

"Okay," he conceded, mind ticking away as he meticulously crawled through our options. "But let's go to the archives first and get to the ninth level, then conduct the reading when we return here. We can gather whatever supplies you need today. If we save it for tonight, and the worst does happen, at least we'll be able to hide out here until you've recovered."

"That's a perfect plan," I agreed, but as we rose and prepared for the day, there was an edge to every one of his movements. His muscles tense, on the verge of that protective instinct; one I worried would only end up hurting him in the end.

Because Fates were unpredictable, and I was at their mercy for the rest of my long warrior life. And Cypherion was willing to position himself between me and the celestial beings if need be.

Chapter Twenty-Two
Cypherion

The temple breathed an eerie stillness against my skin. A handful of searchers knelt in the main room, curtains drawn across nearly all alcoves. The usual pairs of guards drifted lazily down the aisles, mystlight flickering against gray stone where it stretched up, cradling a mosaic across the ceiling.

Everything was in order. I should have been grateful for that.

But instead, unease ticked away at my mind. Mentally, I took stock of my weapons, remembering where each knife was sheathed. The ones against my ribs would be the most discreet and quickest to pull.

The stained-glass windows cast pools of rippling blue light across the floor as I followed Vale toward the archives. Without a word, she slipped away to distract the guard again—a different one tonight, thank the Angels—and with the aid of two thin knives, I had the lock open within seconds.

Could this defense be any more pathetic? Why weren't these locked magically if they were truly to be kept secret?

Then again, numerous acolytes were allowed in here. Why have a lock at all if so many keys were given out?

Shrugging off the criticism of the Starsearchers, I ducked through the archway. My heart pounded as I waited.

When Vale finally slipped through the sliver of moonlight gilding the floor, I thought back to the way I'd surprised her last night when she arrived and how hard my cock got with only the gasp she'd elicited.

We didn't have time for any of that tonight, though.

Vale's gaze was dragged down that staircase, her hands flexing at her sides.

"How do you feel?" I whispered.

She may insist on returning, but if she froze again, I wouldn't hesitate. I'd get her out of here through whatever means possible. Whatever answers the archives held weren't worth hurting her.

She looked over her shoulder, eyes alert and jaw tense. "I'm fine."

She wasn't, though. Now that she'd admitted the pressure her magic had been exerting on her, the tells were clear. She blinked rapidly with a hand against the wall, like the power was trying to force her into the depths of the stars and she needed to ground herself.

But she wanted to be here, and she deserved that choice.

"Let's continue," I said, rolling my shoulders to dispel the uncertainty stiffening my entire body.

As she nodded and turned back, her cloak—the one I'd given her from the Castani market—slipped over her shoulder, exposing that silver tattoo. And even in the dim light, it pulled at me like a calling card, igniting the anger in my chest.

I pushed it away.

On light feet, we crept toward the mouth of the spiral staircase. Its descent was just as intimidating as it had been last night. Vale went first, hand clenched on the rail—much tighter than last night. Orbs dropped from the ceiling, the wavering mystlight within paling her skin.

The deeper we went beneath the earth, the more the magic

stored in Gallantia's land wakened my senses. I kept my heightened stare trained on the Starsearcher before me, ears attuned to any unexpected noises. Nothing but silence echoed along the stone.

My gut tightened as we passed the first three levels without issue.

"Wait," I whispered on the fourth landing, gently grabbing Vale's wrist and pulling her to a stop.

I peeked around the corner. A labyrinth of shelves stretched as far as I could see, but no footsteps echoed between them. No acolyte was stationed at the central desk. Just pale mystlight bathing empty aisles and the flickering cracks of fires in the grates.

That couldn't be. Slipping my hand into Vale's with a slight shake of my head, I ducked down the nearest aisle and quietly wove through the rows.

But no matter how far we went—we didn't meet anyone. My weapons itched for me to pull them.

When we reached the end of the floor, I tugged Vale against a shelf and sank low to the ground. I met her eyes, and it was clear we were both wondering the same thing.

"There's no one down here," she whispered.

I peered around the end of the aisle, almost hoping to hear footsteps in the distance or the clink of a guard's armor. "Is there any reason the acolytes would be called away?"

"If there was a celestial event, they'd be called up to read." I turned back to Vale to meet her slightly-hazy eyes. When had that begun? "If it was large enough, they'd be in the courtyard beneath the open sky, not in the temple itself. But there's nothing tonight. Not unless there's a festival we don't know of or an emergency gathering."

"Even if there was an event, wouldn't you feel that pull, too?"

"Maybe, with the way my magic is behaving, I wouldn't notice the difference," she said, tenuously.

"What about the guards?"

Vale swallowed, and it took every bit of my strength to remain focused on the larger mission rather than the nervous bob of her throat. "They could be up there, too."

I dragged a hand through my hair, searching her face. The wide olive eyes and how she bit her lip to keep it from quivering.

"You want to keep going?" I asked.

"I need to," she whispered.

I didn't comment on the fact that that wasn't what I asked. That there was a difference between what she thought she should do and what she wanted.

"Okay," I said.

As we stood, I pulled her closer to me, cupping her cheeks with both hands and kissing her. Her mouth was warm, her lips finally stopping that trembling for just a moment. And for a few seconds, I reminded her—and myself—that neither of us were going anywhere.

We wound back through the eerie fourth level and continued to spiral down the staircase. The lower we went, the more the magic pressed on me. Mystiques were not guiders of magic like Starsearchers. We didn't use it in the same way, but we were still beings wrought of ether and connected to the earth, as all warriors were. Our blood was laced with that call.

Here, though, deep beneath the surface, it was almost like a great beast was stirring. Like it turned its head toward us.

We descended past the fifth level, past the chancellor's secret office on the sixth, where Vale didn't even stop to check that the coast was clear, before flying down to the seventh, and finally hit the eighth. Stronger power crawled along my skin, but still, we saw no one.

Despite the void, I didn't dare speak. Instead, as we crept down that final staircase—Vale practically floating—I considered the way my senses were awakening.

All magic stemmed from the mountains, seeping from the

rocky cliffs and peaks all the way into the earth. It had wound its way into the Labyrinth and the pit in Mindshaper Territory, where Ophelia had been challenged for Thorn's emblem, and we were much deeper now than we had been then. It made sense that the further we journeyed underground, the more that power would stir.

My boots were silent as they hit the ninth-floor landing.

The imbued ink used to etch the Bond on the back of my neck reared its head, and those threads I'd barely been able to reach lately woke. They were searching for their cause, their source of magic to guard and the network of warriors I was tethered to.

As we paused with our backs to the cold stone wall, I couldn't help but indulge the Mystique legacy pulsing within me. I pulled a small dagger from under my cloak, desperate to feel the steel in my hand.

Vale tracked the movement slowly, gaze lingering on the metal for a moment. Then, she lifted her stare to mine.

And what lay within nearly sent me to my knees.

"Vale," I gasped.

The green of her eyes was almost entirely fogged over. Through the haze, galaxies swirled.

She only blinked at her name, her movements slowed. Less present than they'd been even on the fourth level.

"We can't do this." I searched the aisles beyond her. "Just stay here, and maybe I can—I can—"

But what could I do? I wouldn't know what we were looking for in the archives. She was the one who held the malfunctioning magic and connections to the Fates. I was simply here to protect her.

"We have to see this through," she said, voice chiming against rock. We'd be caught for sure. "The Fates demand it."

My hands fisted. The fucking Fates and their entitlement.

"Are they pulling at you, Stargirl?"

She nodded, galaxies swirling with every blink. "They're louder than ever."

And though fear turned my stomach over, this was what we needed. The Starsearcher at the fighting rings had said the ninth level of the archives held Vale's answers. The Fates speaking to her now had to be a part of that. They had to be leading the way to whatever it was we needed.

"Follow them," I told her.

And without even looking that the coast was clear, Vale turned the corner and floated onto the ninth floor.

I hurried after her, scanning the scene. Every damn level looked the same upon first entrance, no identifiers to tell you how deep you were. It was disorienting and would be easy to get lost down here if you weren't paying attention.

But Vale drifted past endless shelves without concern.

My eyes snagged on the untitled books. I supposed that was a different form of defense for their private information. An intruder from a foreign clan wouldn't know where to look for what they sought.

Unless they had the Fates to guide them, like I did through Vale.

Her hands ghosted over each shelf, fingers gently draping across wood and rifling the open books topping the tables at the end of each aisle.

"Where are we going, Vale?" I asked, voice low. The Bond prickled at the back of my neck, the power surging through my veins. My hands tightened around my dagger.

"Just ahead," she said dreamily. A groan worked up my throat at the lack of control this magic forced upon us.

"Hurry the damn Fates up," I mumbled under my breath.

Vale answered in a chilling voice, "The Fates will not be rushed by the impatience of mortal warriors, no matter the promise they retain in their star paths, Mr. Kastroff."

I froze at the way she addressed me.

Speeding ahead, I cut her off and gently grabbed her shoulder, ducking to meet her eyes. Only a swirling force of stars looked back at me.

"What's going on?" I accused.

"It is fine," Vale said, removing my hand. "She is fine."

I didn't get out of her way. "Who?"

It wasn't Vale who answered. "The woman you love."

She didn't give me a chance to respond before sneaking around me and turning the next corner.

"Here," Vale's voice that wasn't Vale's said as she reached a tall door crafted of smooth, polished silver.

"What's in there?" I asked, sticking close to her side.

Vale turned the handle, and the door swung open without even a creak. The chamber ignited with mystlight and—

"What in the Spirits?" I muttered, following Vale as she floated in.

Wherever we were, the ceiling had been constructed to mirror the night sky. Starlight swirled above as if it was a true window, not nine levels below ground. It reflected off the pristine marble floors and through the oval chamber, almost like the heart of a star itself.

Or the heart of a Fate.

In the center of the room, an aged book lay open, incense already wafting around it. The lilac scent was potent.

Vale glided to the center of the thin cloud, kneeling gracefully before the book.

I pulled another dagger, both hands armed now, and scanned the circumference of the chamber as I followed. Once I was sure we were alone, I glanced over the yellowed page Vale studied. I couldn't read it, but I recognized it.

"Do you know Endasi?" I asked.

Vale had never mentioned speaking any language other than the common tongue. I supposed the Fates spoke to her in their own, but that was internal, something born within her. Not a translation to learn.

"Of course I know the ancient Angel tongue," Vale said in

that other voice, flipping the page. "I was there when it was created."

Chills danced down my spine. There was no way...

"What does it say?"

She pulled the book into her lap and was quiet for a long while. My nerves twitched more with each minute.

Finally, Vale's fingers tightened around the leather, and her eyes flashed to mine. Relief crashed through me to see the greens of her irises pushing through the starry haze.

But a hand pressed to her sternum, and with crushing defeat, she whispered, "I have to read now."

My heart pounded against my ribs as if it was trying to jump right out of my chest and reach out to that look of haunted isolation in her eyes.

I crashed to my knees next to her. "Not here, Vale. Remember? We need to get out. Get back to the inn." My weapons and the book clattered to the marble as I gripped her hands and pleaded, "Let's take it with us. Let's take the book and go where it's safe."

Because we didn't know what would happen when she read, but with the way this place was already affecting her—with an impossible voice communicating through her—it was clear the magic was beyond her control.

She shook her head, and while it tore through me, at least it was her eyes looking back at me—her I was talking to. "It won't be safe anywhere, but here it's strong and controlled."

I breathed heavily. There had to be a way.

"Move back from the incense, Cypherion," she said softly but decisively.

The haze thickened around us, coming between us. I shook my head.

"Please," she whispered, determined.

"You're not alone, Vale," I said through gritted teeth. "I'm right here."

"I know." But she let go of my hands.

I rose slowly, retrieving my weapons and stepping back outside of the ring of incense. As the fog swarmed around her, I muttered to the eddying lilac waves, "I'm here, Stargirl. Us against the Fates."

And her head lifted, olive stare locking on mine for just a moment, before stars swirled in her vision once again, and her eyes fell closed.

I prowled along the edge of the dense circle. The incense reached curling tendrils to the walls and up toward the starry ceiling where Vale's face was aimed. A mingling of woody and bitter scents layered in now, too.

She'll be fine, I told myself.

She had not begun seizing yet. This was like the first few times I'd seen her read in Damenal. Lost to the Fates but orderly. Controlled.

This was not the stricken version she'd become in the Labyrinth.

Regardless, I gripped my weapons tighter, not even sure what good they would do. I wished I had a sword or my scythe. Something to channel the power mounting in my veins this far beneath the world.

Vale had been under the reading for agonizingly long minutes when her hands began trembling.

"By the fucking Angels," I growled, sheathing my daggers and diving to her side.

"Vale?" I asked, panicked but gripping her face gently. "Stargirl, can you hear me?"

She didn't respond, lips moving minutely.

Her whole body started quaking. She was too deep. Too far gone.

Panic formed a vice around my throat as footsteps echoed from the main chamber of the ninth floor, and the door creaked open. Darting to my feet and swiping a dagger from my waist, I sent it flying toward the newcomer before I could even think or see who it was.

The man ducked at the last moment, the blade barely skinning the top of his ear. The metal clattered against the stone wall. And when he stood and grinned at me, a growl rumbled in my chest.

"Great to see you again, too," he said, straightening the cuffs of his tunic. "The capital is beautiful this time of year."

Behind me, shock pulled Vale to the surface. Her gasp pierced the fog, soured with betrayal. "Harlen?"

His name barely left her lips before she toppled to the ground.

CHAPTER TWENTY-THREE
VALE

I was used to the Fates floating through my mind. Their voices usually mingled like drops of mist, yet were decipherable. A lighter tone where every word sounded like a laugh for one, a deep and animalistic rumble for another.

Now, though, as I fell into the chasm of magic within me, they shouted. Louder than the sound of the blade Cypherion had thrown, ripping me from that world and back into this one. Louder than Harlen's voice shredding through my sanity and Cypherion's defensive retorts.

The Fates were all I knew.

An amalgamation of all the readings they'd wanted to give me these past months and everything that had been blocked.

They called to me by name, nine voices on a wind. I knew the Fates, had studied them all my life. They were my friends when I had none.

Now, though, despite the fact that I could peel their voices apart like a frayed rope, I couldn't remember their names or the spectrums they presided over. I could remember nothing. It was all consumed by the futures they poured into me.

It was like repeatedly being held beneath water and coming

up for air, the relief filling my lungs, only to be crushed tightly beneath the weight of magic again.

"Where have you been?" I asked the Fates. "What has been keeping my readings from me?"

Stars spiraled above, tails of starfire burning behind them as they swam along a cosmic current. Deep sapphires and navy blues wavered between the voids, looking as soft as velvet as the trails of the stars' paths faded into blurred images.

"Can you tell me of the Angel emblems? Of the Angelcurse?"

A star cascaded through the sky, and in the stream of its fiery-white tail, a reading formed. A face I knew.

"Ophelia," I whispered as her likeness was conjured as clearly as in a looking glass. A second form swept up beside her, the two talking hurriedly even as the image solidified.

"Jezebel?"

The Revered I wasn't surprised by—she was the one I'd been searching for—but her sister...

I thought back to the Seawatcher challenge on those platforms when Jezebel had demonstrated an unseen level of power, commanding the dying spirit of an alpheous. Oh, how there was so much we'd yet to discover about the younger Alabath's fate.

Creeping closer to the image, I picked it apart. They locked hands—no. There was something held between them. A weapon? It wasn't Ophelia's sword or spear. Perhaps it was one of Jezebel's.

Strength radiated between the sisters, bolts of fiery-blue lightning cracking the flat gray sky. In its wake, thick droplets of gold poured from clouds I couldn't see, gilding their skin.

A Fate's voice whispered around me, one that sounded like the moon cleaving apart in the night. "The sisters promised by legend. Constellations foretold of them."

"Constellations?" I asked, as I studied the lack of landscape wherever Ophelia and Jezebel were. Another streak of lightning shattered the shapeless murky-gray world.

"They command the stars to fall and rise," the Fate whispered.

Shivers traveled down my spine, but the voice faded into the blue velvet sky around me, and the trail of starfire wiped away the sisters, whizzing back into the heavens.

"Where were they?" I muttered. My lungs clenched as if held beneath water again.

Until a spark burned to my left, and I whirled to see a second fortune being written—

I gulped down air. "What?"

Titus's form was within the burning frame. I nearly stumbled back a step.

The first time I saw Titus in a reading, I was eight years old. He'd been conducting his own session on the balcony of his manor. He showed up for me two weeks later at Lumin Temple.

In that reading, he'd been lighting incense and candles, staring contemplatively at the stars as he waited for his Fate to come to him.

Now, though, he raged.

The chancellor stormed through the manor, shattering an ancient vase and dislodging a bust of Valyrie from its stand.

"No!" I yelled, lunging for the image.

He littered his foyer with shards of glass, clay, and ceramic, bare feet slicing across the sharp edges. But he didn't so much as flinch.

"Madness will descend upon him," a darker voice, tinged with malice and the secrets the world hid, hissed into my mind. Angels, I wished I could decipher which Fate the voices belonged to as I usually could, but there was too much right now.

"Show me how!" I demanded. My shoulder burned as if my skin was set aflame. "Show me the path he walks to break into such instability."

"You want to see what breaks him?" the Fate asked, voice whistling through me.

"Yes, please," I answered, straightening my spine, attempting to show the Fate the respect they deserved though panic stole through me.

"Look here," the Fate said, behind me rather than within my head this time.

I spun, and saw—

"What?" I gasped.

A silver-framed mirror had appeared. And my image stared back.

"You will be the ruin, Vale," the Fate said. Then, just as the other had, this second celestial voice faded into mist.

And before I could process anything it had just said, my other seven ties crashed into me. Stars showered from invisible heavens, readings burning through their tails of white fire and sucking all the air from the realm.

Six figures burst to light in one, casting beams of power cyclically between them, then sprinkling them among mountain peaks.

In the tail of another star, separate and yet somehow connected, seven figures rose to absorb those drops of borrowed magic. An iron chain strung between them.

In the third trail of starfire, hordes of people stood with their faces tilted skyward. Starsearchers, maybe? Halos framed their heads—eleven stars, with a gap where a twelfth belonged.

Winged creatures soared through another, swooping so low I nearly ducked, though they couldn't touch me.

The fifth reading showed the face of a girl I missed with every sliver of my Spirit. A boy I didn't know followed quickly after, the two intertwined.

Cliffs towered in the sixth, waterfalls carving through their ledges and cascading to the ground, an indiscernible profile within the waves.

And in the last—

Blood.

So much blood coated the world. The cypher trees rose through it, their leaves dyed crimson. The earth shuddered at its touch. Skulls and ancient bones were painted, sand dunes soaked and heavy with the weight of lives. Every star winked out in the sky; every feathered wing dissolved to dirt.

The pressure of so many readings bore down on me. I clasped my hands to my ears to drown out the voices of the Fates, but it didn't matter. They were within me, tangling into a single, relentless ring.

Those voices pressed closer, the brightness of their readings blinding me.

Until all I knew was a ceaseless white light and a high-pitched chiming that echoed in my ears.

Until I thought this reading would kill me.

CHAPTER TWENTY-FOUR
CYPHERION

"WHAT ARE YOU DOING HERE?" I FORCED BETWEEN gritted teeth. "We left you back in Lumin."

"And by some miracle, I own a horse, Kastroff," Harlen responded, rolling his eyes.

"So, you followed us?" I tried to ignore the fact that Vale had fallen silent again.

"Oh no, I was always meant to return here."

"*Return* here?" He lived in Lumin. He told Vale he rented an apartment in the city and had built a life for himself.

Harlen slid his hands into his pockets, scuffing a heel against the marble floor. "My work brings me to the capital infrequently, it's true. But I'd been requested to keep an eye out for her in Lumin," he said, glancing over my shoulder, "and to race here if I had any important information, such as that stunt in the fighting rings."

Harlen's brows furrowed as he tried to see through the fog and dissect what was happening to Vale. But I shifted to the side to block her from view. Though, truthfully, the haze was so thick in here that he probably couldn't even see her.

How was he unaffected by it, anyway?

"And *who* requested you to keep an eye on her?" I asked,

though I was certain of the answer. There was only one man who cared that deeply—twistedly—about Vale's movements.

"Chancellor Titus, of course." He smiled as he said it, and anger flared deep within my chest. It roared through my veins, fueling the power that had festered there since we traveled so far underground.

I charged before Harlen saw me coming.

No blades, just my hand clutching his expensive silver-threaded tunic and my knuckles splitting as they cracked against his jaw.

Harlen's head rocked back, smacking against the wall, but I didn't hear the echo.

All I heard was the way he'd pretended to care about Vale in that orange grove. The way her voice had fought shattering as she grasped for a piece of her old home.

Gripping his tunic in both hands, I shoved him up against the wall, his feet off the floor. The edge of his jaw was red, a satisfying stream of blood trickling from his lip.

"Whose side are you on, Harlen?" I growled, shaking him. "Because you sure as the Spirit Realm had her convinced you truly missed her."

"You think I didn't know where she'd been all these years?" He spat blood to the floor. When he smiled, his teeth shone crimson. "All of us kids knew of the girl the chancellor rescued from our temple. I followed how she rose within his household, became his little pet."

"So, you *were* jealous?" I pressed my forearm to his throat as the haze drifted tighter around us. Spirits, the shit was over-whelming. "Because she was chosen by him over you?"

"No!" he spat. "I was angry because she was the only person who I thought loved me. I'm not as powerful as she is." I narrowed my eyes. "Oh, don't give me that naive look, Kastroff. I know she's special. She was given attention at the temple; even I was smart enough to figure out there's *something different* about her."

So, he didn't know about Vale's nine Fate ties. Despite recruiting him, Titus hadn't shared that with Harlen. Interesting.

"I was a gutter rat found by the temple masters," Harlen growled. "Orphaned and abandoned on the street, but as ordinary as any warrior. *She* was my only friend. And one day she was gone." He heaved a sigh, still pinned to the wall. "When Titus came looking for me in Lumin a few months ago and told me she was imprisoned by the Mystiques, and he thought you might bring her this way for negotiations—when he asked me to keep an eye out, to report to him, and in exchange he'd name me his newest apprentice—it was the easiest choice I've ever made."

Titus spun that fucking story to suit his interests. And named Harlen an apprentice in the process. I didn't want to think about how Vale would feel when she found out.

"Have you considered that perhaps he was only searching for her to hurt her?"

Harlen's eyes widened. "No. He saved her." His stare narrowed again as he pressed against my hold. "*You* are the one keeping her away."

I loosened my grip, letting him slide down the wall but not releasing him. "No. I'm not."

"What are you saying, Kastroff?" His hands dropped to his sides. I scanned him to ensure he didn't have any weapons. Nothing easily accessible at least.

"I'm saying—"

"I believe that Cypherion Kastroff is trying to turn yet another of my warriors against me."

Harlen and I spun toward the door as it swung wide.

And Titus strolled into the chamber.

Silver robes adorned his body, shooting star pin tacking the garments closed at his chests, and square beard neatly trimmed close to his face. The well-groomed appearance as deceptive and poisonous as ever.

"Is that what I'm doing?" I asked, abandoning Harlen and drifting as casually as I could back toward Vale. My heart careened in my chest at the thought of her waking from her reading to the chancellor here. She was so vulnerable right now, and I was meant to protect her.

"Is it not?" Titus challenged, crossing his arms.

"I think we both know who spews lies around here, Titus."

He raised his brows, an impressed smile on his lips at my lack of formality. I'd sprout wings before I showed this man a modicum of respect ever again.

"I operate on what the Fates say," Titus said. "Are you accusing celestial beings of lying?"

Something about his words piqued my attention, about the way he'd structured that sentence. *I operate on what the Fates say.*

Not on what his readings tell him.

Not on what is shown to him.

What the Fates say.

It was an odd way for a searcher to reference their power. Vale always spoke so personally of hers, like each session—even those that ended poorly—was an intimate experience. Like they were the cosmos woven in the sky, laden with complex mystics and futures that weren't fully understood unless you were the one to see them.

Titus spoke analytically, as if the Fates could be coldly classified. Another clan's magic perhaps but not how one typically spoke of their own.

"Titus—"

But before I could raise any questions, something pinched my neck.

I reached up, finding a small needle in my skin.

And I collapsed to my knees as the chamber faded.

Chapter Twenty-Five
Vale

When the Fates finally released me from their timeworn grasps, my body was wrung out and heavy. More so than ever.

Sensation returned to me slowly, but I was on my back, chills peppering my skin.

It took a few tries for me to regain control of my body. Was this because I'd forced my magic down for so many weeks? Likely.

Finally, I tentatively flexed my fingers at my side, searching for anything to grip.

Where I expected to meet the cold stone of the chamber floor, I found soft fabric beneath the pads of my fingers.

My eyes flew open, and I rocked upright, my head spinning. As my vision steadied, a cry lodged in the back of my throat.

A silver and diamond chandelier looked down from the center of the room. The light was caught by sweeping, dark curtains pulled across the windows, stretching from high ceilings to rug-covered floors. Because as a girl, the starkness of the white stone flooring had reminded me too much of the temple.

I was on a bed much too large for one person, set in an ash-white frame with four posts and silk curtains meant to signify luxury, privacy, and intimacy. Things I'd never realized I didn't feel here.

And a skylight revealed the heavens, storm clouds blocking out the stars.

I was back in my room in Titus's manor.

"No." My chest splintered.

I stared at the roiling sky above, a cold emptiness stealing through my body. In my mind, a future was torn from my grasp, leaving my fingers raw and bleeding from trying to cling to its broken edges.

I'd been returned to my cage, and instead of the affluence and safety I once saw it as, cold bars rattled as they slammed shut, snuffing out my freedom.

I stood at the glass door to my balcony for a long time. Too long, probably. I wouldn't open it, though. Wouldn't attempt to go outside. Because I had a sinking suspicion that the door couldn't open. If I didn't try, at least I could live in the denial that it was my choice to remain behind the glass.

My room was on the third floor, elevated above the rest of the First District and giving me an expansive view of Valyn. Storm clouds blocked the moon, the capital unspooling at the foot of Titus's manor and forming a wave of deep shadows and flickering mystlights.

They almost looked like stars poured onto the street, the world turned upside-down since Cypherion and I entered the archives earlier this evening.

Cypherion...Every time I thought of him, his name tore through the splintered hole Titus's betrayals had ripped within me. I pulled my velvet cloak tighter around my shoulders.

Where was Cypherion? Hopefully not here.

I hoped he ran. I hoped he abandoned me in that temple

when Harlen showed up. Pressing my hand to the cool glass, I hoped he was far away now.

Though it wasn't smart given recent events, a piece of me wished I had reading supplies so I could search the Mystique Second's fate for any indication that he'd gotten out of the archives. But apparently my room had been stripped of anything useful in the months since I'd been gone.

When had that happened? Was it following the Battle of Damenal, when I revealed I'd been the one to read the darkness shrouding Ophelia during the Rapture last spring? Had Titus stopped trusting me entirely then, or had it taken more time to devolve?

Perhaps it was only recently, once word reached him that I was back in Starsearcher Territory and had not come to him?

Perhaps he'd never intended for me to return here at all.

The readings I'd seen of him destroying priceless artifacts and ancient works of art played through my mind again. What would happen to shove the chancellor I used to admire into that madness?

It was possible he'd been on that road for much longer than I cared to acknowledge.

The door to my suite swung open, and I whirled, half expecting to see Titus striding in here, pretending to be relieved and charmed by my presence.

It wasn't him, though. An unsettling disappointment swooped through me. How was I still so dependent on Titus's approval after everything I'd acknowledged about him?

A question for a later time because the person entering my chamber had a heat rivaling starfire churning in my gut.

"What are you doing here, Harlen?" I sneered. "Why in the everlasting Fates are you working with Titus? And *how*?"

"Vale, are you all right?" He strode confidently toward me, as if he was allowed access to my bedchamber without question.

"Now you care?" I asked icily, lifting a brow. I crossed my arms to keep myself from hitting him.

Harlen flinched. "I have *always* cared about you."

"Enough to lock me up." The reminder had my fingers curling into my velvet cloak. My throat tightened.

Taking a slow breath, I looked up at the skylight and tried to pretend I stood in my hot springs, nothing but trees and a star-speckled sky for miles. I imagined the scent of washed stone and bergamot, the warm water lapping at my bare skin and steam wafting through the air, curling the tendrils of my hair along my temples.

"That's what you think I did?" Harlen asked, exasperation pitching his voice and breaking my meditation.

I closed my eyes and said goodbye to that safe space amid the jungle.

"It may not seem that way to you. But look around." I turned back toward the balcony doors, Harlen following. "I am *not* free within these walls." I placed one hand against the glass. "These views may be freedom for some, displaying the world and dreams waiting beyond, but I feel them like slices against my skin."

His brows pulled together. "What are you talking about?"

"I have *always* been a prisoner here." I glared at him, voice low. "I didn't realize it for many years, and my life here was certainly better than in the temple, but there were common rights I was still not granted. Things I didn't even think to ask for after living in fear."

Harlen scoffed. "I heard of your triumphs, Vale. Of how you were named the youngest apprentice in Starsearcher history, most likely to take Titus's position decades from now." He stepped closer, but I didn't retreat, only kept one hand against the glass. "How you were his precious little *pet* he paraded to the Raptures."

Understanding ignited a flickering spark in my brain. "You're jealous?"

Harlen was quiet, his lips pressing together exactly as they used to when we were children. His hands fisted at his sides.

Sixteen years may have passed, and yet Harlen had all the same tells.

He likely had the same desires, too. He was trying to fill that basic need for affection, for nurturing and unconditional love. The things we'd both thought Titus was giving me as a girl—a father when I had been ripped from mine too young.

Harlen had missed me when I left Lumin, and he had allowed bitterness to fester in the space I left behind.

Though I was wary, I understood how that could happen. We had only been children after all. And it was that mental image of a younger us, so hopeful about getting away from the temple, that dulled the edge of the anger within me.

"Harls," I sighed. "I missed you every day of those first few years here. And then, as I grew older, I convinced myself you were better off at the temple without me. They never wanted you for your magic the way they did me."

His head tilted curiously.

"I told myself our paths were better unwound," I continued. "You would not be dragged down by the possessive battles over my magic."

"I don't understand, Vale. What do they want with your magic? And what was happening in that chamber when I found you and Kastroff?"

Cypherion's name sent another pang of longing through me. I didn't know what he'd said to Harlen in that chamber, but there was a waver of wariness through my old friend's voice that convinced me he was trying to see my perspective, to see the walls of this manor for the cage they'd become.

And if I wanted to stand a chance of ensuring Cypherion was safe, I *needed* Harlen on my side.

I chose a truth that was solely mine—nothing to do with Cypherion's friends—and shoved aside the lingering distrust.

"I have nine Fate ties, Harlen."

He froze. When he spoke, his voice was quiet, like saying it too loud might summon the celestial beings themselves. "Nine?"

"Nine," I confirmed. And I prayed to all of them I hadn't just made a horrible mistake in revealing this.

I told him how the Lumin Temple council had found out I was powerful and stole me from my family. How I'd thought Titus was my savior, and how I only realized recently that he was far from it. How my readings had been malfunctioning—though I left out Ophelia's Angelcurse—and that was why Cypherion and I were sent here.

Harlen asked many questions—he was always a curious little boy, now a studious grown man—and I answered them as best I could without exposing the Mystiques' secrets.

And when I finished, we sat before the fire in silence for a while. Finally, Harlen asked, "How can I help?"

Determination hardened his expression, thawing a bit of my wariness. All he'd done—while it was unknowingly betraying me—had been to help me, after all.

And I did not have to trust him in order to work with him. If his goal was truly to help me, this was a mutually beneficial partnership.

"Cypherion," I finally breathed, his name desperate as it left my mouth. "He got away from the archives, right?"

Harlen sheepishly said, "He's in one of the guest chambers on the second floor."

Of course he hadn't left. He hadn't left *me*.

I fought back the stinging that rose to my eyes at that understanding and pictured the layout of the manor, the vast halls and endless rooms he could be in. Some cold and empty, some lavishly furnished. I had an inkling which Titus would have given him.

"Hurt?" I asked.

Harlen swallowed. "Drugged." The world nearly exploded around me, and I shot for the door. Harlen stopped me, grabbing my shoulders and looking in my eyes. "It's leaving his system. He was just starting to wake when I came up here, but you can't go to him, Vale. Think of how Titus would react knowing your first move when you woke was to seek out the Mystique?"

Not well, that was how. But— "I don't give a star-damned fuck what Titus wants anymore, Harlen!"

"I know, I know," he soothed. "But if you want Kastroff to live, we have to be smart."

"To live?" I muttered.

"If everything you've told me about Titus using you is true, and he lied to me to recruit me so easily, I can guess what lengths he'll go to keep you here." Harlen's words settled in my gut like stones sinking below a pond's surface. "If he thinks Kastroff is a threat to that..."

He could order him to be tortured. Or worse.

I nodded, trying to stifle my panic and gripping my velvet cloak tighter around me. "Is he chained?"

"Just restrained with ropes so he couldn't attempt anything when he woke."

That was good. Ropes shouldn't hurt him, and it would likely settle him a bit to know they hadn't shackled him. Cypherion was strategic enough to know that had to be intentional.

"I need him to be okay, Harls," I whispered, my lips trembling as I forced the words out. "Whatever happens, I need him to be okay. He saved me."

Harlen pulled me in for a hug, and this time, I allowed the comfort. I pressed my hands against his chest and took deep breaths in time with his. When I stopped shaking, he mumbled against my head, "You truly care for him?"

"More than the Fates could have foreseen," I admitted.

"That won't go well." There was an apology in his voice that resonated deep in my bones.

I pushed back to look up at my friend. "I know, but I—"

"No, you don't understand." He shook his head. "Titus

says you *belong to him*. Not as an apprentice. As property, like it's tied by magic or something."

Unease snaked down my spine, but in its wake, indignation rose. My spirit reared within me as if lit by the hottest starfire the Fates could muster.

"I am no one's property," I ground out. I'd once belonged to someone, to a master and an age-old structure.

Never again.

Never again would I be at the mercy of *anyone*. My choice was my power now.

"I didn't realize how the chancellor viewed you when I signed a contract with him," Harlen said. "I hope you can believe that."

And though I remained wary of offering him trust, to an extent, I did. He had betrayed me, but Harlen had been as damaged as I was by the temples. I didn't think for a moment that he would support the chancellor demanding ownership of me or any other warrior.

It had been the lost boy within Harlen making that misguided deal to save the friend he missed.

Taking a step back, I sank onto the edge of my bed.

"How did it happen?" I asked. "The contract."

"He preyed on my weakness." Harlen shrugged and sat beside me, bracing his elbows on his knees. "Said you were in trouble and that you'd asked for *my* help. You were like my sister, Vale. I couldn't leave you. He told me the Mystiques held you prisoner and that he suspected you'd be returning on orders from the new Revered, but only briefly." He folded his hands, fingers fidgeting. "Titus wanted me to help you get away from your guard and return you here so he could protect you. And he made me an apprentice in exchange for my help."

An apprentice. Another stinging betrayal against the wounds in my heart. I was so imperative yet so easily replaced.

I shook my head. "He was never the one protecting me."

But even as I said it, a twisted feeling wrenched through my gut.

"I see that now. I saw it when the Mystique threw that knife at my head." A sly smirk twisted his lips. "That was not a body-guard protecting his prisoner. That was...something deeper."

"I need to see him," I said, spinning on the bed and tucking my legs beneath me.

"I don't know if it's a good idea."

"Please, Harls. Bring him here. I won't ever leave my room." It wouldn't appease Titus, but at least if he thought I was staying where he wanted me, I could spin that obedience in an argument. "And then, we need to get him out. Can you help me?"

I didn't ask about myself. I knew where tonight ended for me.

"Fine." Harlen sighed and strode to the door. "Dinner will be in an hour, though. We'll have to be quick. Wait here."

"Okay," I said, fidgeting with the edge of my cloak.

As he gripped the door handle, Harlen turned over his shoulder. "I'm sorry, Vale. I was only trying to protect you."

I gave him a tight-lipped nod. Not forgiveness, but partner-ship. "I have learned to be my own protector, Harls."

"I'm proud of you for that." His eyes shifted to the wardrobe beside the balcony doors. "He'll want you to change, you know. That cloak...it will only anger him more."

Then, he was out the door, and I was left staring at the wardrobe, dread hardening in my gut.

Chapter Twenty-Six
Vale

"Vale!" Cypherion tore into the room with none of the cool collection I'd grown to expect from him.

I looked over his shoulder at Harlen. *Get him out tonight*, I begged with one last look at my friend. He nodded and left, pulling the door closed so Cypherion and I could have a moment of privacy.

Then, I scanned my warrior. His hair was half pulled back, but the ends looked gnarled, like fingers had clawed through them. Dark circles framed his eyes after waking from whatever drug they'd used on him, and his clothes—the same leathers he'd been in when we went to the temple—were disheveled, not a weapon in sight.

The frantic search of his eyes around my bedchamber froze me to my spot before the mirror. As he peeled back the layers of the life I once led here, stripped down to its bare minimum, an uncomfortable vulnerability settled over me. He was seeing a person I used to be.

Cypherion studied the room for a long, quiet moment, while my heart thundered, and pressure built behind my eyes.

Then, his gaze landed on me. On the only dress that had been in my wardrobe. A silver fabric that shimmered like it was woven with starlight, crystals lining the fitted bodice. I'd had to lace it as best I could on my own. Dainty straps wrapped around my shoulders, and the skirt flowed to the floor, full but deceptively so, with high slits slicing up to my hip.

Cypherion swallowed as his eyes tracked over every inch of my body. "You look…"

"It's the dress Titus left for me."

"Then it's the worst dress I've ever seen." But with the way his eyes dragged over it, burning with desire and heady need, it was clear that was far from the truth.

And despite the nerves crashing through my chest and the tears stinging my eyes, my lips twitched up slightly and a watery laugh bubbled out of me.

At the sound, Cypherion swept across the room, his arms wrapping around me. "Stargirl," he breathed, bending to kiss me.

I wrapped my hands around him, digging my fingers into the curls at the back of his neck. Grounding myself with him.

He pulled back quickly.

"Are you okay?" he asked, cupping my cheek and letting his gaze drop down my body. "Have they done anything to you? Harlen said you spoke…"

I could see in his gaze that he didn't trust Harlen. And I didn't blame him.

"I think he's on our side here," I said. "He was lied to as I was. And I'm fine." I didn't add that while I was okay physically, being back here was like tugging a vital piece of myself away. A piece that had learned to hope and dream and choose.

I thought he knew regardless.

"We're going to get out of here," Cypherion promised. "We just have to go to this dinner first."

"I don't think you should come," I said. "Harlen said he'll help get you out."

Cypherion argued, "I'm not leaving you. I promised I won't let anything happen to you."

"I'm fine."

"Stargirl"—he sighed—"don't lie to me."

I didn't respond.

"We'll go to this dinner. Then, we'll get out of here." His words came out rough and desperate, a bit turned up at the ends, like we both knew there was a very good chance he was wrong. "We'll play nice, be diplomatic. But I can promise you the Revered won't allow us to stay here a moment longer than is necessary to keep peaceful standings with your clan. When my letters stop arriving, Mystiques will be beating down the door to this manor."

He sounded sure about that last part, but with each word, my heart only cracked further. Because he may be a Mystique, a member of Ophelia's council, but when it came down to it, I was a Starsearcher.

Under Titus's jurisdiction.

I swallowed that truth.

"It's going to be okay," I said.

He is going to be okay.

A tear snuck out the corner of my eye. Cypherion caught it, tilting my chin up, his other hand snaking around my waist.

"Tell me what I can do, Vale." He gripped me tighter to him. "Please, whatever it is. Tell me what you need."

"You," I said, hollowly. Clinging to him, I dragged my lips over his jaw. "Remind me what it is to feel beyond these towering walls."

He turned his head slightly, and his lips melted against mine, a slow answer to my desperate question. Then, the need ignited between us.

Cypherion scooped me up and carried me to the bed. Placing me down gently, he hovered over me with his elbows on either side of my head, caging me in a way that somehow made me feel more free, more alive.

As his lips skimmed my jaw, I widened my legs on either side of his hips so I could feel all of his weight against me, his heart beating against mine through our clothes. Locking one leg behind his back, I pulled him closer.

"What do you want, Stargirl?" he breathed as his mouth worked down my neck, erasing my worries. "Anything you want, all of me. It's yours."

My head fell back, heart beating faster with each press of his lips against my skin.

"Please," I begged and rocked my hips against him. "I just need you now. Need you to remind me." Remind me of the world beyond this manor and all we'd fought through to get here.

Cypherion braced a hand beside my head, looking into my eyes. He searched for something I wouldn't let him see.

"Are you sure?" he asked, brushing a strand of hair behind my ear.

I nodded. "Positive." It wasn't a lie, and I was glad he didn't insist I talk about why I wanted this so desperately. What I was preparing for.

Instead, he pulled me to my feet and untied the bindings of my gown, letting it sink around my ankles.

"Horrible dress," Cypherion said as he wrapped his arm around my waist and lifted me back onto the bed.

"Hideous," I muttered against his lips. Frantically, I unbuckled his leathers, and he tore off my undergarments.

We didn't take our time, didn't stop to indulge. He was plunging into me with one quick thrust, and the pleasure of being with him drowned out the fear of what came next.

He dragged his hips back, snapping forward and watching me for even the smallest reaction. Timing his movements to wring the highest amount of ecstasy from me. When a moan slipped up my throat, he held my hips at that angle to continue driving into me with perfect pressure.

"Cypherion," I gasped, reaching for him. He dipped his head to capture my lips with a searing kiss.

"That's right, Stargirl. Just us. No one else fucking matters." As if to seal the point, he thrust punishingly.

Cypherion interlocked his fingers with mine, bringing my hand to his mouth and kissing it. Then, he placed it on the bed beside my head as he pounded into me again and again, every stroke hitting deeper.

I memorized the feel of his hand in mine. The image of him above me. The way sweat glistened across his brow and his abs contracted with each movement.

"I love you," I whispered.

And Cypherion didn't hesitate. "I love you, too, Vale."

He kissed me, one hand still locked with mine, the other holding my hips in place.

And as I tumbled over the edge, and my heart stopped racing afterward, he held me tightly. "You're never going to be at his mercy again so long as I live," he promised. "You may be in this manor, but something is different this time."

"What?" I asked.

"You're not alone." He kissed the tattooed brand on my shoulder. "It's us against the Fates, Stargirl."

And because of the raw conviction in his voice, I didn't tell him that I feared he was wrong.

It was not us *against* the Fates, but us living in the wake of everything they'd already planned.

CHAPTER TWENTY-SEVEN
CYPHERION

TWO GUARDS KNOCKED ON VALE'S DOOR TO ESCORT us to the dining room. They didn't seem the slightest bit surprised at finding both of us in her bedchamber.

We were dressed, sitting in front of the balcony doors she refused to open as I asked her to recall her favorite moments from this spot. Storm clouds rolled over the city, dark and heavy and foreboding, and Vale told me of a festival day where she sat on the balcony with one of Titus's staff, and the girls shared some of the recreational rolled herbs she'd brought to Renaiss all those months ago.

It had been tranquil for a few moments.

Now, as we walked closer to those towering, gray wooden doors of the dining room, the manor took the image of a prison. The angles of every corner seemed sharp enough to kill, the planes of each window an unbreakable barrier.

The guards left us at the door, and Vale lifted a hand to the shining silver handle.

"Wait," I whispered, grabbing her wrist. Her skin was cold. "How do you want to play this?"

"What?" Her eyes searched mine, lined in such a dark blue it was nearly black. As she tilted her head, the shimmering powder atop her cheekbones caught the light. She shone like a gift from the Fates, my Stargirl.

The contrast of her dress against my leathers was not lost on me. She was the Starsearcher darling, beloved and cherished, and I was the brutal guard who had been keeping her from Titus.

That was his story, at least.

"How are we behaving in there?" I asked. "I don't want to make Titus angrier." Not if she would catch the consequences of his fury. "Do you want to play into his game?"

She blinked those wide olive eyes up at me for a moment. Then, she slipped her fingers between mine, locking our hands together.

"He no longer writes my fate, Cypherion."

And without another word, she shoved open the door to the dining room.

But there was a certainty in her voice that didn't match the hollowness of her stare, one that sent a chill of unease down my spine as we faced her captor together.

The walk to the long rectangular table was endless. Vale's heels echoed louder than seemed possible on the marble floors, sound carrying between the limestone pillars lining either side of the room and bouncing off the windows at the opposite end, up to the arched ceiling.

And standing before those windows, watching the wind whipping against the glass with his hands behind his back, was Titus.

He didn't turn immediately, and each moment he waited, wrath boiled in my gut. My grip grew tighter on Vale's, but she remained steady.

As we reached the end of the table, I squeezed her hand, and we both stopped. This may be Titus's manor, his land and jurisdiction, but there wasn't a chance we were getting closer without at least some acknowledgment.

His story of me being nothing but a guard aside, I was the

damn Second to the Revered Mystique Warrior. I'd earned a modicum of respect at least, and I'd enforce that title if it meant helping Vale. Spirits, I'd wear the damn thing proudly.

I allowed it to straighten my spine now, assuming the authority of a leader.

We would not stay in this manor a moment longer than was necessary.

Finally, after the silence of our halted footsteps broke through his facade, the chancellor turned. His navy silk robes were a thick brocade, lined with silver that matched Vale's dress, and nearly had a growl rumbling through my throat. They were no political pair to be paraded around.

Titus ran a hand over his neatly-trimmed beard, raising his thick black brows in fascination, and a sickening smile spread across his face.

"Welcome home, darling!" he cooed.

I bit the inside of my cheek to keep from snapping. My free hand automatically reached for a dagger, but they'd been taken, my sword and scythe still back in the attic room of the candle shop.

Vale flinched at his greeting. Only minutely, as if she was stifling the reflex or some force stopped her.

"Thank you, Chancellor," she said, her high, clear voice ringing like a bell. So demure yet strong.

"And Mr. Kastroff." Titus nodded at me. "It's a pleasure to see you again. Though I wish the circumstances of this reunion would have been better coordinated."

"Or it could not have occurred at all," I said blandly. "We each have our preference, it appears."

"Yes." Titus grinned. "It does appear so."

A weighted silence hung between us all.

"Well," the chancellor said, "why don't we sit? No point standing about when dinner has been prepared and we have so much to catch up on."

I led Vale around one side of the table, pulling her chair out for her, but halfway into her seat, she froze.

"Why are there four place settings?"

My head snapped up. Spirits be damned, I was so distracted by Titus I hadn't even noticed.

"I thought it would be wrong to keep this dinner just to us." He sneered as he spoke—just barely—but I caught the accidental twist of his lips and the threat threaded through his words. "We must include your ally."

As if on cue, a side entrance to the dining room opened, and Harlen strode into the room. His gait was strong, confident, but mystlight shone across his face, and a freshly-blooming bruise mottled his cheekbone.

"Harls!" Vale gasped, standing up with palms braced on the table.

I placed a hand to her back, glaring at Titus. "What did you do to him?"

"He needed a reminder of the contract he signed." He shrugged, and worry squirmed through my gut. Had Harlen told Titus anything about Vale?

"Are you okay?" Vale asked, gaze still locked on her friend.

"I'm fine," he assured her. His eyes begged her to sit, to obey what was being commanded.

It made me sick to consider, but this was the chancellor's game. Even if Vale said she would not succumb to his plans for her, we had to tread carefully.

With a gentle squeeze of her hip, I tried to communicate that I agreed with Harlen. Reluctantly, Vale sat. I claimed the seat beside hers, Harlen across from us. Titus took his time settling into the head of the table and fanning his napkin across his lap.

The chancellor snapped his fingers, and staff members filled the plates before us. But I barely even looked at the food or the wine they poured. I kept my glare on Titus and imagined every creative way I could end his life right now.

"This is lovely," he said with a content sigh as the servers cleared the room.

A clap of thunder echoed over Valyn. The storm's prickling tension bled through the glass windows and stone walls, settling over the table and testing my sense of control.

"What is it you want, Titus?"

His brows rose at my lack of decorum. No title, no false niceties.

"I don't recall you being the one with a brash temper, Mr. Kastroff. That was Mr. Vincienzo, was it not?"

I thought back to the Rapture when Tolek had sternly spoken to the former Mindshaper Chancellor, Aird, for how the man addressed Ophelia.

"I suppose I just needed the right motivation," I said with a shrug.

Titus smirked, smug. "You know, when word first reached me that you were in my territory, I assumed it was in search of that emblem your Revered hunts."

"A task you have yet to assist with," I reminded him. The chancellors—all but Aird, who had died during the Battle of Damenal—had each agreed to assist with finding the shards of their Angel's power.

"Have I not?" Titus crossed his arms, leaning back in his chair.

"Not in the least." I bristled. He hadn't written a damn word to Ophelia regarding the Starsearcher token. Only that he had people *working on it*, as requested, but after so many months of silence on various alliance efforts, we suspected it was a lie.

"Regardless"—he waved off my accusation as if the emblems were inconsequential—"after what Harlen witnessed in Lumin and what occurred last night, it seems there is something else at play here." Titus turned his attention on Vale. "What is happening with your readings, darling?"

I followed his gaze to the Starsearcher beside me. Under the table her hand sought mine.

Vale bit her lip as if fighting some words from bursting. Her fingers fidgeted.

And then, an explanation bubbled right out of her like the clouds cracking open outside.

"My magic is malfunctioning. It's been happening since Daminius, and the episodes have only gotten worse. I haven't had a clear reading in months, and when I try, I faint."

Titus's jaw ticked. For the first time tonight, he wasn't the one holding control. "You should have come home sooner."

"Home?" Vale scoffed. Her grip grew solid in mine. "You *left me*, Titus! I wrote to you every week—sometimes every day—after Daminius, when I was no better than a prisoner of the Mystiques, begging for you to get me out of there. And how many letters did you write back?"

Titus was silent, searching for an explanation he either didn't have or was reluctant to give.

"That's what I thought," Vale spat. "I knew the letters returned weren't from you. Did you think I wouldn't recognize the handwriting as someone else's? After being your apprentice for *years*?"

"Darling—"

"I do not want your excuses," she said, voice lethal. "I won my way out of that cage with honor. I became a true ally to the Mystiques, and in turn, they are helping me decipher what's wrong with my magic."

Pride burned through me at how she spoke. That was my Stargirl, as fierce and strong as the constellations that lined the heavens for eternity and burning just as bright.

"How could you abandon her like that?" I added. Titus glared at me. "If Vale is as important to you as you say—"

"I would never truly leave her," he interrupted my accusations. I wasn't sure what he meant by that, but my attention piqued at the knowing tone of his words.

"Vale," he said, addressing his apprentice again, a new desperation seeping through her name. "You should have come back sooner. I have resources to help you."

"I put it in the letters," Vale admitted. "I asked for help." Her voice broke over that last word, a crack in her armor.

"And speaking of her readings," I added, "why were you two not affected by the incense in the archives as she was?" Both Harlen and Titus seemed unbothered while Vale was overtaken by…something else.

Titus answered, "Typically, a Starsearcher can postpone a reading at a given time. What happened to Vale is likely a result of her Fate ties being so powerful. And so stifled."

Did that also mean that strange voice that had overtaken her was because she'd been succumbing to so much power? That thing that claimed it was there when Endasi was created?

Titus addressed Vale. "I'm guessing once you succumbed, they were a flood. I didn't know what was plaguing you," Titus admitted. He was somewhere between wrenching sadness and the edge of force. He was ready to push her into accepting his excuses, and that grated on my restraint.

"Why wouldn't the stars have guided you to help her?" I accused.

"The—"

"Fucking Angels," Harlen gasped. All heads whipped toward him. I'd nearly forgotten he was here, but now the Starsearcher was gaping at his chancellor. "Your sessions don't work, do they? You can't read a damn thing."

Silence crashed over the room, so deep you could hear a coin drop on the marble floor.

"You never…" Vale began, voice trailing off. Her lips moved, but nothing came out.

"What wild accusations are you brewing now, Harlen?" Titus spewed. His glare locked on the Starsearcher.

Harlen didn't fidget, his eyes didn't waver. He pushed up from his chair and planted his hands on the table, tilting his head so his fresh bruise caught the light like a beacon. "Something with your magic doesn't work."

My mind spun, hand tightening on Vale's under the table.

Titus's brows flicked up. "And why do you think that?"

"Because you've never shown evidence of any kind of session you conduct," Vale blurted, staring at her captor with a deeper betrayal in her eyes. "Ever since I moved here, you used *my* sessions. My readings were the ones you reported to council members."

She spun to face me. "At the Rapture last year. That reading about Ophelia was mine. The one that promised darkness and destruction across Gallantia."

She'd confessed as much after the Battle of Damenal. I braced for the wave of deceit that reminder would drudge up, but it never came.

Instead, I met Vale's eyes and confirmed what she'd shared with us all those months ago. "It's true," I said. "At the archives, you said you *operate on what the Fates say*. Not what your readings show you."

The choice of his words had stood out at the time, and I'd been about to ask him what he meant before he had Harlen drug me covertly.

"All these years," Vale said, "have you ever had something to share of your own or has it all been mine?"

"And since I signed that contract, he's used mine," Harlen added. The disgust was thick in his voice.

"By the Angels," I mumbled.

"Do you have a Fate tie, Titus?" Vale asked, voice softening a touch for a reason I couldn't make out. Absently, her hand that wasn't holding mine massaged her shoulder. My eyes narrowed on that spot.

"Of course, I have a Fate tie, darling," Titus said.

"But do they show you anything?" Harlen asked, leaning forward. His eyes were wild with a manic energy.

"Tell us the truth, Titus," Vale pleaded. "Or neither of us will read for you."

"You both will read for me, or your magic will rebel against you."

"Torture us for the damn readings, then," Harlen spat. "Do your worst, Titus, and we will withhold."

Vale nodded, and by the fucking Spirits, I thought they meant it.

Titus ground his jaw, backed into a corner by the two warriors he'd come to rely on. The two his own greed and fear had pushed him to manipulate. "My Fate does not show me as much as others show their tied."

Which, if his sour tone indicated anything, meant nothing at all. The chancellor had such a weak alignment that the stars barely showed him any readings.

With that confession, a chill seeped into the air. Rain lashed at the windows, and silence filtered around us.

"How did you come to hold your position, then?" I asked.

"I worked for it, Mr. Kastroff. Not everyone receives things because they're blessed by the Fates or Angels. That is an anti-quated way to distribute power, don't you think?"

I didn't respond, because in a way I agreed. I didn't hold any special magic or Angel blessings, yet I held a title. And against this man—this sham of a leader—I did so proudly.

"I climbed up the ladder of authority," Titus continued. "First in my school years, then serving in our army, and finally, in the political world. I have conquered all of it—*earned* all of it."

"Then why lie?" I asked. Beside me, Vale stewed silently.

"Because our people rely so heavily on their precious stars. I have lived my entire life with little power and have plenty to show for it. But it comforted them to remain with the familiar, so I recruited those who could aid me."

Recruited those who could aid him...

"Did you instruct the temples to collect children who

showed promise?" My voice was as sharp as a blade, one I longed for right now as the chancellor shrugged and smiled smugly.

Vale and Harlen both froze.

"You *what*?" she asked, voice small. "You're the reason they took me from my family. The reason they beat us into training our magic properly."

"I needed to track those who would be of assistance to me, darling," Titus said, eyes only for her again. "I didn't know they would do those things, but I needed to find you so that we could take care of our people."

If he was truly as appalled by the disgusting behavior as he should be, he would have enforced punishments on the temple masters.

Vale shook her head, not saying anything, like she recognized the lie, too. A broken look slid into her eyes.

I pushed up from the table, and Harlen did the same. "Vale and I will be going. Harlen, you may come if you'd like." He was already rounding the table to join us. I bent to whisper in Vale's ear, placing a hand on her back. "Let's get out of here, Stargirl. He's hurt you enough."

She only shook her head more, a war behind those shell-shocked eyes. It tore at my heart, squeezed it to pieces where she held it in the palm of her hand.

I couldn't read her. Beyond devastating hurt, I had no idea what was going through her mind. Like that hollow look she'd had in place before we entered the dining room had siphoned away all of her emotions.

"Actually, you won't be leaving." At Titus's voice, my head snapped back up.

"You don't own them, Titus," I spat.

"You are technically correct, but I do have these."

From beneath the table, he removed a set of scrolls. Even from here, it was clear the parchment was worn, the ends tattered. And their presence alone weighed the room down with an atmospheric pull, like the center of a whirling vortex or a black hole in a star-flecked sky.

"What are those?" I asked, narrowing my eyes on the scrolls.

"These are from Valyrie's personal collection," Titus explained of the Starsearcher Angel. "You accused me of not aiding Miss Alabath in her hunt for these emblems. Well, that is false."

He waved one scroll at me, stamped closed by a silver seal. He had been searching after all—but he'd been saving the information as leverage.

"What do they say?"

"These here are precious Starsearcher records. Legends of readings Valyrie and her closest warriors conducted. I believe that in here, your Revered will find what she needs, if she knows how to look. You may even find some other very interesting bits of Angel tales that relate to those you care about." Titus leaned across the table, placing the three scrolls in an untidy pyramid. "You may take these when you leave." His eyes sliced to Vale. "*Or* you may take her."

Damien could have fallen from the sky before us, and I wouldn't have moved in that moment.

My world shattered, the crash echoing through my head. Or perhaps it was my spirit breaking, rage flooding the cracks at Titus trying to manipulate us all like this.

"Keep your fucking scrolls, then," I hissed. "We'll find another way."

Vale's voice was delicate, tenuous as she whispered, "Cypherion—"

She sucked air between her teeth, grasping her shoulder again.

Her hair slid across her back, thin lines of silver catching the light between her splayed fingers.

My eyes flashed from that ink to the man responsible.

And the nameless thing always bothering me about the tattoo finally made sense.

"You've fucking tied her to you haven't you?" My voice was ice cold, even to my own ears, a contrast to the fury burning through me.

"*What*?" Harlen roared.

"The ink you used on her tattoo over the brand," I accused. "It's imbued. It's why she was so drawn to your fucking office in the archives. It's why she's been struggling so hard to grasp this tainted hold you have over her. Because there's magic in that tattoo that makes her come back to you."

It was why she'd been so adamant that Titus was good, why it had been so hard for her to name his actions for what they were even after she knew. She likely would have struggled with it either way, having been manipulated by him for so long, but she kept coming back to his defense. Kept being magically dragged to that office in the archives.

The betrayal was rotten either way, but this violation of her free will made it even worse.

"No..." Vale said, but it was the kind of denial where it was clear she understood the truth. "How *could* you?"

"We'll discuss that later, darling," Titus said. Then, he looked at me. "Now that you see that she can't get away regardless of what she does, I suggest you take these." Carelessly, as if they weren't crumbling and containing legendary secrets, Titus pushed the scrolls toward me. "Come on, Mr. Kastroff. Don't you want her to heal her magic? I am the only one with the resources to do that."

It was evident he didn't care about the scrolls, the Angelcurse. Likely didn't even care about Vale's magic beyond using it. All Titus was concerned with was himself. He'd clawed his way into this position after unlikely odds, and now he would do anything to retain it.

But *I* would do anything for Vale.

Not for her magic, but for her happiness. For the freedom she craved and the safety she deserved.

I didn't care what revenge Titus got for this, what treason

he accused the Mystiques of. Vale would not stay in this manor another day. I wouldn't force her back into a cage she'd worked her way out of, take away the liberty she'd begun to crave. We'd find a solution to her malfunctioning power some other way.

I'd watched her come back to life these last few weeks, and I would put a dinner knife in Titus's chest before I allowed him to clip her wings. I eyed the table, wondering if maybe I could pull it off before he called his guards.

But Vale's voice sliced through my thoughts. "Cypherion." Before I even met her eyes where she was still seated, I knew what she was going to say. And just the preparation for it was like my heart being crushed. "You have to go."

The actual words hurt even worse.

Chapter Twenty-Eight
Vale

"No," Cypherion argued immediately, dropping to a knee. The others in the room fell away, only him before me. "Vale, I won't leave you."

Call it intuition, but I'd known walking in here I wouldn't leave with him by my side. Perhaps it was the stars giving me time to prepare, so I could send Cypherion away with confidence rather than letting him see my distress.

Titus had welcomed me home today, but home was no longer a place. It was the man on his knees before me now, his pleading stare searing my spirit.

"I'll be okay," I promised, taking his hands between my own.

"I swore to you—" He stumbled for the words, his voice low but jagged. "I swore you would never be at his mercy again."

"I won't be," I corrected, though the thought of staying here wrenched through me like a poisoned root tearing up the soil of my dreams. "No one owns me, Cypherion. But I am choosing this. I am choosing to stay here both to find the answers he says he can offer about healing my readings, but also for you."

"You can't do this for me," he rushed out.

"You need the information in those scrolls, Cypherion."

"Stargirl—"

"Your *family* needs this information." It was twisted of me to pull that string. Pitting his love for me against the love for his family, for the people who had been at his side for a decade. But I didn't care. It was the one card he couldn't refuse.

"I don't want to choose them over you." Resignation roughened in his voice. He was losing this battle.

"You're not," I assured him. And truly, I didn't feel like he was.

They were the pillars of his life. Cypherion wasn't himself without the people he loved. If they were gone, he crumbled.

Me? I was simply standing on that platform at his side, greedily leaning into the strength they gave him. Place me somewhere else, and we would still exist.

We would. I was certain of it.

I allowed myself one moment. One moment to sink into the sadness staring back at me from his blue eyes. One moment for despair at this decision—at being within these walls—to wrap around my gut.

Then, I shut it all down and put up the guard we both needed.

"You're not choosing them over me," I repeated, willing Cypherion to hear the truth beneath my words. "And *I* am deciding my fate this time. I'm staying here of my own free will. I will heal, and I will become a bigger asset in this battle with the Angels."

And then, I would free myself of Titus's clutches for good. I would rip the chains from his hands and wrap them around his throat, crumbling his rule with them.

Cypherion swore I would never be at Titus's mercy again, and I wouldn't. The Chancellor of the Starsearchers would be at *mine*.

"I'll be back for you." A pang went through my heart—through both of ours, I thought, judging by the crack in his voice. "I'll be back with a way to break the bond in that tattoo, too."

There was no way—tattoo bonds went soul-deep and could not be undone—but the determination in his voice almost convinced me there was.

Cypherion looked over his shoulder at Harlen, and it wasn't a question when he said, "You're staying here."

Harlen nodded, committing to remain with me in this manor, no matter what it meant. Cypherion took a breath as he faced me again, convincing himself that was a small comfort and not misplaced trust. Stretching up, he pressed his lips against mine, sealing that promise between us.

"It's okay," I swore. I brushed his hair from his eyes, my hand landing on his cheek and his head shaking ever so slightly. "It's okay."

Cypherion stood, pulling me to my feet and into his arms. He looked over my head, fingers curling into my back. "I swear to the Angels and Spirits, Titus, if you harm her in anyway, you will be drawing your own death. I know your secrets, and I'd thoroughly enjoy making it a long, torturous end fit for the crimes."

I didn't turn to see how the chancellor blanched. Didn't need to with the chill from Cypherion's voice seeping into the air.

And I had to curl my fingers into my palms, dig my nails right into my very flesh to stop them from trembling against his chest, because he'd notice. Those little hints of fear, Cypherion would notice them.

He'd know I was not entirely okay remaining here. That my chest was cracking, my heart strangled by fear.

But I was staying regardless, even if it took years for this war with my magic and hunt for the emblems to end. I was not okay returning to my cage, but I would do it to claw my way to fair freedom. One without fear shadowing me as it had since I'd stepped back into this territory.

"You go to them, now," I said. Cypherion's heart broke in his eyes, but I swallowed back my tears. "You go, and then come back for me."

When he kissed me, I savored it. Memorized the taste of him, the way his lips commanded mine expertly, and the feel of his heart hammering beneath my palm. Remembered how it had felt to be with him one last time in my bedchamber and how he'd held me.

"I'll be back for you, Stargirl," he whispered. "I promise. Not even all nine of your Fates could keep me away."

"I love you," I said.

"I love you, too. Guard up, Stargirl."

And then, he grabbed the scrolls and left, not looking back, because we'd both buckle if he did. As he disappeared, a hollowness filled my chest. A chasm his presence had repaired, one that fear sank its claws into once I no longer had to maintain a front to force him away.

And a sob fought out of my throat as the bars of my cage slammed shut once again.

But this time, despite my dread, they rattled. Fissures pierced their iron reign over me in the shape of a captor's lies, an ally's schemes, a warrior's love, and the absolute power of nine Fates.

"Come, Vale," Titus said, turning to the table. "Let's eat."

Harlen eyed me warily.

"As we must," I muttered.

Now that I'd been out—now that I'd experienced the truest form of desperate, all-consuming love—the weaknesses in this enclosure were evident. I noted each, and I began to plan their demise.

Titus might have shattered every promising bit of starlight

within me—might have broken me—but now, I'd return the favor.

Now, I would become the breaker.

WANT to read the hot springs scene from Cypherion's point of view? Download an exclusive bonus chapter now.

ACKNOWLEDGMENTS

This book was supposed to be a short and sweet little story that would fill in some character activities that come into play in the future. When I set out to write it, I didn't realize how much Cypherion and Vale would latch onto my heart or how deeply those hooks would sink. So the biggest thank you goes out to them for sharing their story with me and allowing me to tell it.

Of course, I have to thank my family first as always. I'm truly so lucky to have such a great support system (though Dad, I really hope you skip the pages I tell you to skip this time...you don't need to support *everything*). And to my friends, thank you for being so encouraging of my dreams and never missing an opportunity to brag that I'm an author, even when I won't. I promise I'm coming out of my writing cave (and I mean it for real!).

Thank you to my phenomenal editing team for their work on this book. To Friel, Kayla, and Len–extra thanks for how excited you were when reading and all the hype about Cypherion and Vale. And a huge thanks to the artists who have brought this book to life, especially to my cover designer, Fran, for another phenomenal cover. Every time I don't see how they can get better, yet you amaze me! Thank you to my agent, Ezra, for being so excited for everything that's in store for the Gallantian Warriors and beyond, and for being such an enthusiastic champion of my career.

As I've said before, I am incredibly fortunate to be in the indie author space. I've made some of my closest friends from this community, and I don't think I'd get through the day without them. To the coven, the indie goddesses, and all the others who have even just dropped one DM or comment my way–thank you. And a special thank you to Liz, Chey, and Carmen for the endless love and reminders that I'm really doing this.

Thank you to the beta readers who took time out of their busy lives to provide such valuable feedback on this book. One day, I'm going to treat you all for all of your help! And of course, to my street team and all of my ARC readers. There are so many days that being an author is as draining as it is fulfilling. Every mention or reaction in Discord is a sign to keep going. This series would truly be nothing without you all.

Finally, to you. For continuing on this journey of myths and fate and fighting for love. You're all warriors at heart, and I'm so honored to have you here.

Infinitely yours until the stars stop shining,
Nicole

Nicole Platania was born and raised in Los Angeles and completed her B.A. in Communications at the University of California, Santa Barbara. After two years of working in social media marketing, she traded Santa Barbara beaches for the rainy magic of London, where she completed her Masters in Creative Writing at Birkbeck, University of London. Nicole harbors a love for broken and twisty characters, stories that feel like puzzles, and all things romance. She can always be found with a cup of coffee or glass of wine in hand, ready to discuss everything from celebrity gossip to your latest book theories.

Connect with her on Instagram and TikTok as @bynicoleplatania or on nicoleplatania.com.